Gwendoline Butler

A NAMELESS COFFIN

CT Publishing

First published in Great Britain 1966

This edition 1999 CT Publishing.

Editorial Consultant: John Kennedy Melling

A CIP catalogue record for this book is available from the British Library.

ISBN 1-902002-11-3

9 8 7 6 5 4 3 2 1

Book design and typography by DP Fact & Fiction

Printed and bound in Great Britain by Caledonian International Book Manufacturing, Bishopbriggs, Glasgow.

This book is fiction. All characters and incidents are entirely imaginary.

A NAMELESS COFFIN

Chapter 1

AGENDA FOR the Burgh Court of Murreinhead, Angus, Tuesday, May 12th, 196-.

(Notes made for his own convenience by Giles Almond, Writer to the Signet, Notary Public, countryman and author. Almond, as Clerk, was responsible for convening the Burgh Court.)

Adjournments

(These made up a good proportion of the Burgh Court's work. Magistrates' courts have to put up with many more delays than the higher courts. Witnesses fall ill, move away, get lost, or simply fail to appear; inquiries have to be made about the defender's character, or the police asked for more time. Giles knew this well, although he often reacted impatiently. Yet it was all work to him.)

Summary Offences

Indictable Offences

Deposition of Absent Witness

(Sandy Shaw had emigrated to New Zealand but was still required to tell what he knew about the night the Baillie's house was broken into. In the opinion of the police, and others, Sandy had taken himself neatly out of trouble.)

The list was pretty much the same as usual. Adjournments were more common than usual owing to the illness of one of the magistrates, Lady Rose Rayburn.

Giles Almond had scribbled a note of the names of magistrates whom he might call upon to attend:

Mr James McGinn

Mr Daniel Blair

Mrs Martha Gilchrist

Dr Alexander Paton: sprained his wrist while out shooting but will presumably attend as can still ask questions, in fact more talkative than ever, and hates to miss a session.

Sir James Gemmel

Finally Giles had written for his own attention a few notes on a current case:

Mrs Robertina Louden or Dean against Mrs Elizabeth Hamilton or Robertson. Mrs Louden charges that Mrs Hamilton slashed her best coat with a knife on the back and below the pocket while pressed against her in the crowd coming out of the Bingo session. Lizzie says she didn't for she was never near Mrs Louden and she never had a knife.

Robertina Louden is thirty-five. An attractive woman.

Lizzie Hamilton is fifty if she's a day. Her husband works at the Mill.

Chapter 2

WHEN DOES a case begin? When the idea of crime first comes into the criminal's head? Or when the act itself takes place? Or when the police first get to hear about it? Or is it less tangible than that? Is there a subtle shading off, so that ordinary, careless, selfish behaviour slides over the line and becomes anti-social and criminal? Is this why the Devil got his first big casting as the Serpent?

There was a huge new supermarket in the main road in Coffin's manor. Six months ago it had opened on the site of an old cinema. On a corner with a factory and a block of offices opposite and a hospital next door, it was well placed for custom. In fact it was a popular, cheerful place and was soon absorbed as an institution into the life of the neighbourhood. You could park the baby in his pram and drink coffee in the patio on the ground floor. At rush hours there was even a distracted nurse to watch the babies and separate the dogs. There were always dogs, tied to the prams or wandering in and out or anxiously trying to get into the main shop after their owners. A large printed notice declared that Dogs were not Allowed on the Premises, but it was an ineffective prohibition. The store manager used to dream of the coming of a dogs' Pied Piper. His other dream was that he was a dog, and was running round barking and fouling the shop. After nights like these

11

the notices about dogs were always made bigger and more numerous. On this hot day in late April they stood about eighteen inches high and were as thick on the walls as graffiti at Pompeii. But still no one read them.

Most of the shoppers were women, but there were usually a few men and boys among them, looking lost amid their purposeful and pushing sisters. A few of the women were shabbily dressed, but times were prosperous, and the majority wore pretty dresses and smart handbags and shoes.

Between five and five-thirty on that same afternoon about fifty or sixty women with their children, handbags and shopping passed through the cash desks. It was just past the peak hour, and housewives were rushing home to start the evening meal.

About half of these women—twenty-five or twenty-six of them: it was not possible to be precise about the number—discovered when they got home that their handbags were scratched. Some bags were deeply scored, others had received just a tiny little mark, nothing more than a nick. One or two women probably failed to notice that there was anything wrong with their bags at all. The rest blamed their own clumsiness.

None of the women realised that she had been the victim of an attack. Not one knew that she was a *victim*.

It was a horrible summer, day after day of steady heat, which made the pavements livid and dirty. Londoners even began to think wistfully of grey skies and rain. The sales of aspirin and sun-burn lotion went up. Milk turned sour, butter was greasy, and the food in the shops looked dry and stale. The grass in the big parks was brown and trodden into dust. People sat about in their gardens, at the windows, and on the pavements. There was no privacy anywhere.

"We shall have trouble," said John Coffin, Divisional Detective Inspector (hoping for promotion: hadn't he been a good clever boy lately?) for a South London district, gazing out of the window and thinking of the large area he was responsible for, containing houses, shops, factories, docks and one huge comprehensive school.

"I don't know why it hasn't started yet." John Coffin didn't believe in the Devil and the Serpent, but he knew all about crime and a lot about wickedness, and he was learning more every day. He stared at the heat shimmer. "This is the sort of weather the Great Plague must have flourished in," he felt gloomy and unwell himself, and would have liked a good cry, but men weren't allowed to do that sort of thing. Instead he kicked the table and glared at his assistant. "Trouble," muttered Coffin. He looked at the telephone and waited for it to ring.

The telephone was quite silent, as it had been for some time. This was in itself unnerving. "All dead," he muttered. "All dead. Sitting there, hunched over their telephones, all dead." A picture came into his mind of dead people crouched over telephones in rooms all over London.

"Don't you believe it," said his colleague Sergeant Dove, who was not imaginative. Although the sergeant was unimaginative, he was not without the usual burden of introspection and anxiety. Not for nothing was he called Dove. There were swarms of Doves in the district. Many times Coffin had thought that an anthropological survey of his district would make fascinating reading. It was a neighbourhood in which four great family groups still predominated in spite of war, rebuilding and social planning. Nothing any Council planner could do would efface the power of the Stones, the Doves, the Dinebons and the Whitechairs. You still came across these names in every housing list, every school register and every cemetery in the district. They were on both sides of the law, some were honest, some were not. Fred Dove was a policeman. His remote cousins, whom he did not as a matter of fact yet know and who lived down by the docks, were just opening up a line in stolen cars that was shortly going to introduce him to them. There were certain common physical characteristics. The Stones were shortish, solid-boned, but with neat hands and feet; the Doves had poorer physiques, and a tendency to hypochondria (in which Sergeant Fred Dove, not otherwise a typical Dove, shared: he was at this moment wondering if that pain was an ulcer) and were well known to all the local doctors and hospitals; the Dinebons were large and quiet, so good with their hands that they had once produced the best forger in Europe; and the Whitechairs all had sharp blue eyes and a strong sense of justice which naturally often looked to their friends and neighbours more like a sharp sense of grievance. The Whitechairs marched in protest, went on strike, and organised mutinies as the decades and centuries rolled by. They had been among the Londoners who egged on the Peasants' Revolt in the fourteenth century and enrolled Chartists in the nineteenth. They were often on the losing side but turned out indestructible in the end.

Coffin himself had a streak of Whitechair blood in him. At the moment, oppressed and uneasy, he felt sure there must be a Dove gene or two loose in his blood as well.

"Anyway, we've *got* plenty of trouble," said the sergeant, looking round at the files around him.

"Yes," said Coffin, in a dissatisfied way, as if he wanted more and worse trouble. Then he smiled. "Don't think I'm greedy, Fred." The same Christian names came up time and time again among the Stones, Doves, Dinebons and Whitechairs, and Frederick was far and away the favourite, whether because it had a fine imperial ring to it or because an extremely successful local boxer had been called Fighting Fred Fisher. Coffin was never sure. "I'm not really looking for trouble. I just feel it coming," he settled down to the work on his desk.

Coffin was looking for trouble which carried a gun or killed a child or strangled its wife or burnt down its neighbour's house. His district had had plenty of trouble of this sort over the last decade, but trouble rarely comes wearing the face you expected.

Out in the hot streets, crowded with shoppers and idle walkers escaping from their houses in search of moving air, the knife was already known, had already established its reputation in a quiet undercover way, but no one had thought to mention this to Coffin yet. No one had even told the police.

A long thoroughfare ran through the heart of Coffin's district and went down almost to the river. Half-way along, just where Creevey Buildings stood on the corner of Courcy Street, this road widened enough to contain barrows and street traders. On all weekdays, except Monday, which was a dead day, there were fruit and fish stalls, and at the weekend on Friday and Saturday the fruit stalls were joined by traders in cheap dresses and fabrics, shoes, handbags, stockings and large pale-faced dolls. This bustling energetic market was dominated by a large public house called the Red Bull, hence a trip to the market was known locally as 'going up the Red'. Everyone went up the Red sooner or later. Coffin had done it often himself although as a policeman he was hardly a popular figure there. Changes in social habits, prosperity and the well-designed cheap goods to be bought at the huge chain store just opposite had not really diminished the Red's popularity. The women of the neighbourhood enjoyed picking over the articles laid out on the stalls and bargaining with, and insulting, the traders. Their grandmothers had done it, they had heard their mothers do it and they meant to do it too. The stalls offered good value. They had to; competition was so fierce. Some of the things for sale were stolen property. The police knew it and the shoppers probably knew it. But to buy these things was part of the fun and part of their curious attitude to law and order. A long history of civilised and restrained urban life lay behind them. In spite of all the pressures of disease, poverty and war over the centuries, they had never gone quite so far as to court bloodshed, or shoot anyone at the barricades; and now they queued politely at street corners for buses. But behind this carefully evolved feeling for social justice was a dislike of authority. Coffin realised this as well as anyone, and knew that combined with a real sense of the value of law was a strong desire to put the police in their place. It was often catch as catch can in Courcy Street and Creevey Buildings and among the crowded stalls of 'The Red'.

This partly, but only partly, explained their attitude to the knife.

Out of Creevey Buildings, which was a tall grubby block of flats built in the late nineteenth

17

century by a philanthropist grown rich on the slums around the Tower and river, came a solitary dog. The building was being cleared of its inhabitants. Demolition was due to start next month. Almost everyone had already gone, only one old lady clung on in her rooms on the ground floor with seven empty and derelict floors above her. The local authorities and the police had more than a suspicion that a West Indian family were illegally camping out on the sixth floor and a certainty, so far unproved, that the men who had raided the bank across the road three days ago had used the third floor of the Creevey as their observation post. On the very top floor of all was a tenant who came and went and whom no one so far knew about.

The dog turned the corner and trotted off down Courcy Street. He was living free in the Creevey too but he was a lawless quarrelsome hound who had never had a home and never wanted one. He was off now to steal some food from a steak and sausage shop he knew of in Lower Dock Road. He was limping a little. On his back leg was a long thin scratch which must have been deeper than it looked to impede him so much. It was almost as if he had been slashed by a knife.

The demolition men were in for a shock when they came to knocking down Creevey Buildings. Although the structure looked so derelict, it was really immensely strong, with thick walls and tremendous foundations. Architecturally it was

18

something between a prison and a fortress.

"They say the rats'll swarm out of there when they knock it down," said the newspaper man who sold his papers on the corner opposite.

"Go on," said his customer, who was leaning from her ground-floor window to reach for her paper. The houses faced right on to the road on that side with no front garden and no railings; it had its advantages. "I hope they don't come my way then."

"Oh no, they won't stop here. They'll go straight down to the docks," said the newspaper man seriously. "That's where they'll make for."

"With the Pied Piper, I suppose?" said his customer, sceptically.

"They've got a rats' highway through to there," said the old man with a rapt secret look. "They know the way. You won't see them go, though. it'll be at night, with no moon, and the King Rat will lead them."

"I don't know where you get hold of all this rubbish," said the woman, turning round and preparing to draw down her window, "but if you think there's anything in it, you ought to tell the Sanitary Authorities and have them fumigate the building." She shut the window with a bang.

"They could skitter down this road and go straight to the docks and get on a ship and go to the Indies, Scotland or Scandinavia," said the newspaper seller dreamily. He stared down the straight road. Very distantly, he could see the funnel of a ship and the top of a loading crane. He had never been any nearer although he had lived in the district for forty years. He lived and worked and moved in a small area bounded by four roads. Outside them he was a foreigner.

But the idea of the rats had liberated his imagination and set his mind on its wanderings.

"There's boats down there that sail off to Scotland, Iceland and America," he said aloud.

"I've never seen any rats," said the woman, suddenly drawing up her window and popping her head out, "but if it's true, then they ought to burn the place down."

"They'd get out," said the newspaper man dreamily. "You can't stop a colony of rats. Colony," he said again, as if he liked the word.

"You were going on about the pyramids and the Second Coming last week, now the rats," said the woman angrily, slamming down her window again.

"It's the same thing," he said, with a rattle at her window. "That's what people like you don't understand."

He arranged his papers carefully on her windowsill and left a plate for people to put pennies into. Then he went off down the road to drink some lemonade at a café there.

Between Creevey Buildings and the Red Bull, where the stalls thinned out and finally stopped altogether, was about five hundred feet. Along this short stretch of pavement the crowds were so thick they could hardly move on this hot afternoon. Friday towards five o'clock was always a busy time.

One woman was standing on the edge of the crowd, studying them closely, turning her head this way and that to take everything in. She had bright, slightly protuberant eyes that moved restlessly from person to person as if trying to assess each person's movements. She was thin, almost emaciated, but quite smartly dressed in a cotton dress and white shoes. She had no handbag but she was clutching a bundle of shopping in her arms.

"Not buying anything from the market today, ducks?" called out the nearest salesman.

"I have bought already," she said bleakly, never taking her eyes off the scene in front of her. Her sharp gaze did not miss the figure of the newspaper seller on his way to get his lemonade.

"Old loony," she said spitefully; she was always cuttingly contemptuous of anyone she thought abnormal, not a proper person, as if to emphasise the gap between them. Perhaps because she feared she really fell into the same class with them and there was no gap at all. "*He* couldn't have done it though. Not clever enough. Takes someone sharp to do that to me."

It was her belief that it would take someone very clever indeed to rob her as she had been robbed. Her use of the word sharp was unconsciously significant. A knife had helped to rob her.

She stood there now, studying the crowded street, trying to pick out the person who had taken her bag.

"Because he'll do it again." (If it was a man. It

21

could equally well have been a woman.) "It won't just be me that was robbed of her handbag. He'll try it again and I might catch him at it," her pride demanded that others should suffer too. *She* wasn't going to be the only one caught.

All the time she stood there brooding over what had happened to her, her body was making minute muscular movements as if acting out the scene again. All through her thirty odd years she had fought her own battles and she meant to go on fighting them now. She didn't trust anyone else. "Better lose a character than a pound note," was her cry. Her character had gone long ago. But like a cat she had more than one character to lose: a character as a daughter, as a wife, as a mother, as a woman. One by one they had all gone. Now she had nothing left to maintain but her character in her own eyes as a sharp woman.

An hour ago she had started out to buy a new dress in the market, her brown handbag hanging over her arm, a newspaper held in her hand, and wearing dark glasses. Perhaps she shouldn't have worn dark glasses, perhaps it had made all her faculties less keen, made her less aware of the body that brushed against hers and the hands that came too close. She lifted her lips in a thin, tight, sardonic smile.

She had gone into one end of the market with her brown handbag containing over ten pounds and she emerged at the other end with a cheap cotton frock in her arms and with a handle hanging over her wrist.

A sharp knife had cut away her handbag.

She almost thought of the knife as having a separate life of its own.

But she was not going to report the matter to the police. In this behaviour she had good sound reason. Reason of character, reason of circumstances, both weighed with her, and she did not distinguish the two. To her, circumstance *was* character. She was an outsider, she stood a little way from the social group she now surveyed.

"What would the police say to me if I complained of being robbed?" She laughed silently. "Probably tell me I'm fair game," her eyes flickered so hostilely over a passer-by that the woman moved hurriedly away. "I'm not one of *them*, and they know it."

Slowly she walked from end to end of the market ending up not far from Creevey Buildings. The heat did not inconvenience her, she liked it, she was one of the few people out that afternoon who did. The smell of the dusty streets, the heat, even the crowds all had an exotic appeal to her. She was usually happy in this street, like a tourist on Broadway or on the Boulevard Haussmann.

"They can tell lies as well as anyone, can't they? I'll look after myself, thank you."

She looked pugnacious, and you suddenly saw that, cornered, she could be a very ugly customer indeed.

But although she patrolled up and down for some time longer she could see no trace of the bag-snatcher with the knife. Presently even her determination became discouraged, and she turned the corner of Courcy Street, set her face towards the docks and disappeared.

A mean-featured, ferret-faced little woman darted out of the crowd and placed herself against a shop window; she was followed by an older woman moving more slowly because she was heavier and also, burdened with a loaded basket of shopping in each hand.

"Oh, stop panting like that, Mother."

Her mother did not answer at once. Finally after taking several puffing breaths she said in a sort of gust: "You take the bags then."

"I can't, I can't. Oh, I'm in such a state."

"You're a fool, my girl."

"It's too late for that sort of talk, Mother."

Her mother inhaled deeply.

"Pat your pockets to see if it's in one of them."

"I haven't got any pockets. Do talk sense, Mother."

"Pity we never bought that dress we looked at."

"Shut up, Mother."

"At least we'd have had the dress... It must have been when you opened your bag she saw how much money you had there. *That* was your mistake."

"We don't know it was a woman."

"There was only women round us."

"Then perhaps it didn't happen at the stall. How

can we know? I looked down and the bag was gone. Cut off," her face was white.

"I told you not to flash that money."

"Oh, come on, Mother. I'll think of something."

Her mother put down the loaded baskets. "No. Let's stay here for a bit."

"Don't get difficult, Mother. I can't stand it if you're going to be difficult."

"I have plenty of friends, dear."

"You *are* being difficult."

"Ten pounds, was it, Doris?"

"Twenty." There was a farmyard resemblance between them, and if Doris looked like a ferret her mother was more like some larger placid creature, say the aurochs, more given to painful and unpleasant ailments like Bang's Disease or the bloat. Oddly enough she was more like a bull than a cow, something like a Dame in a Christmas pantomime.

"We can tell the police," she said, watching her daughter.

"No. I'm not telling them about this money. Jim gave it to me special and he wouldn't want me to go to the police about it."

Their eyes met. They both knew that there were one or two ways in which cash came into Jim's pockets that neither the Income Tax authorities nor his employers the Dock Labour Board knew about. It was warm money that slipped greasily through their hands. Usually they got something for it, but sometimes, as now, it disappeared in a way they could not account for. It certainly wasn't lucky money.

"No, we'd better not say anything. Mum's the word." She was fluent in out-of-date, half jocular slang, leaving the impression that there had once been a world of cheerful, not too scrupulous comrades in which the old woman had moved easily.

So by the time Coffin sat in his room worrying about trouble to come there had already been at least two, and possibly more episodes concerning a knife, of which no one had complained and of which he had heard nothing. But this situation did not last much longer.

At five-thirty on Friday, May 15th, a woman pushing a pram and holding the hand of an older child, suddenly set up a great wailing and crying that her handbag was stolen. Both her children started to cry too. A small crowd soon gathered to help and sympathise. An older woman fetched a policeman.

"What's the matter now?" he said patiently. He too felt the heat and was in the mood to be patient but not energetic.

"I've been robbed. My bag's gone." She was in tears. "And look," she pointed to her coat. "My coat's been cut too." There was a long slash by the pocket.

She had no hesitation in telling him all about it, but she knew so little. She had been occupied with her shopping, the baby in the pram and the other child. She could remember nothing which would

26

cause her to look back and say: Yes, that must have been the moment when it happened.

Within the next half-hour a young girl indignantly reported that her yellow plastic pouch bag had been slashed from her shoulders. The thief had got her week's wages, and, what she valued much more, a signed photograph of John Lennon. She was philosophical about her loss.

"I can get another one, though, I know the way. I'd had it a long while, it was a bit cracked across the nose. Anyway, I think I'd like to move over to The Monsters now." She was a young girl who liked to keep up with the pacemakers in her world. "I've got ten pounds saved up. I'm not worried about the money. I just shan't have to buy my pair of cork-soled clogs this week and perhaps *next* week they won't be all the glass, so I won't have lost anything anyway. Anyway, I reckon it's the biggest glass of all to have your bag snitched," and she danced off. But she was the only one who had any information to offer.

By the early evening of the next day, Saturday, May 16th, some half-dozen similar cases had been reported to Coffin.

And now he *had* a bit of trouble to get on with, Coffin wasn't grateful at all.

"I hate these knife cases," he grumbled. "The knife slips or gets too sharp and what have you got?"

There was still plenty known about the knife and its activities that wasn't getting through to Coffin.

27

Many local people knew, and Coffin didn't, that there were at least two women who had discovered knife marks on their handbags but who for some reason or other still had the bags. They also knew of one woman who had a torn coat and said this had been cut by a knife. The word went round that the criminal was not a professional and probably not a local. Soon it was common talk that crimes of this sort often led to something nastier. People felt as if they had seen the entrance of a new strange character on to their stage. A skittery amateur with quick hands for a knife was not welcomed. In its way the neighbourhood had nerves.

"Six bags and over sixty pounds in two days," said Coffin. (Here he was wrong, of course, in this as in other matters the police information was not complete, the thief had had nearly a hundred pounds.) "Well, there's one thing: if he keeps it up at this rate, we shall soon have him."

But in this too he was quite wrong. There were no more cases next day nor next week and for the moment it looked as though everything was over.

One other incident took place on this hot weekend in May, which was certainly recorded by the constable on the beat which took in Courcy Street and Creevey Buildings, but to which Coffin's attention was not directed.

Late on Saturday night, but still well before midnight, the constable was stopped by a woman who told him she could hear sounds of fighting in the little alley that ran beside Creevey Buildings back in the direction of the river.

She corrected herself. "Or anyway sounds of shouting. And I heard a woman scream." She had put on her coat and hat to come running out to the police but she was still wearing her bedroom slippers and she was beginning to feel embarrassed by them, and by the policeman's way of seeming reluctant to believe what she said or to take it seriously. Fights were not unknown around here on a Saturday night. "I was just going to bed."

"How long ago was this?"

"Just now. I came straight away. Except for putting on a coat." She stared down at her pink fur slippers: she seemed to have forgotten her summer straw hat with the daisies and roses on top. "Perhaps you ought to call it more like a struggle than a fight," she said in a worried voice, studying his face.

But when the policeman went down Mowbray Alley flashing his light, he could see nothing at all, no signs of a fight or a struggle. Everything was still and empty. Only a cat lurked in the shadows.

The policeman turned back, and put everything down to the imagination of his woman informant.

Perhaps in Creevey Buildings a light flickered high up on the sixth floor as if a candle or a torch had moved there. But there were still secret inhabitants behind that Gothic facade sprung from Jeremy Bentham's 'New Prison' out of *Nightmare Abbey*.

In a small back street about half a mile away from Courcy Street and the Red Bull one old woman, who lived permanently in an invalid chair at the window of her sitting-room, was saying good-bye to another old woman.

"Bye, Lal," said the second old woman, who was as bright and active as a bird. "See you tomorrow."

"Usual time?"

"Usual time."

"I don't know how you can bear to be alone in your house Winnie," said Lal as she watched her friend go. "And your eyesight's getting so bad."

"I don't know how *you* bear the crowd you've got here."

"Ah, but it's company, and I need company."

"Of course you do, Lal. Sorry I spoke."

"Not that I actually see much of them. But I *hear*."

"I should think you could hear that dark chap that has the drum and the electric guitar and the dustbin lid."

"Yes, I do hear him. And the three lads on the floor above. It's company, though."

"You need a woman near you, really," cried Winnie, though conscious as she spoke of the delights of being brisk and energetic and on your own two feet while Lal, who had always been the stronger and the braver, was laid up. Winnie was also thinking of the quiet pleasure of her own tiny house waiting for her. "I mean, just for company."

"I've got you."

"Yes, but I mean at *night*. That's why I've got my lodger."

"Well, let's hope the next one is better than the last one, then," said Lal. "For she was never there, was she?" She was thinking what a fool Winnie was not to know a bad lot when she saw one. Surely that one *was* a bad lot?

"Not much," said Winnie.

"I say, do you think she's...?" And Lal looked down her nose as she hinted.

"Not in my house!" said Winnie sharply. "Goodbye now. See you tomorrow."

"I suppose you *did* give her notice?" said Lal.

"Good-bye," said Winnie.

"Usual time," agreed Lal. "See you tomorrow." But Winnie never came. All next day Lal waited.

She waited and waited, but Winnie never came.

Chapter 3

IN MURREINHEAD, Angus, it was less warm than in London, but still sultry and stuffy. The refreshing east wind which usually blew had dropped. By late evening the town centre was almost deserted. Giles Almond could look right down the street from his sitting-room window and see no one. He preferred it that way.

"There isn't a handsomer curve or a better looking street of houses anywhere in Europe," he said lovingly, letting his eyes follow the gentle slope of the street and the facade of handsome stone-built houses. He himself lived and worked in such a house, one of the oldest, if not the very oldest in the town and built by his paternal ancestor in 1790. The date was above the door and the name, Giles Almond, Writer to the Signet and Notary Public. With very few intermissions, there had always been a Giles Almond to succeed him. "It's never dull in Murreinhead. Sometimes maddening, but never dull and always beautiful."

His eyes fell on a figure quietly walking down the street. Lizzie Hamilton going home to bed.

"Lazy old besom," said Giles under his breath. "For all she looks so neat and canny." His face looked exactly like the Raeburn portrait of his great-great-grandfather as he passed this judgement. This earlier Almond had been raised to the Bench and had sat in the Court of Session at Edinburgh. Giles, who looked so like him, was not ambitious of becoming a judge. His aims and hopes ran in a different direction.

The street scene made a better composition with the figure of Mrs Hamilton neatly placed two-thirds of the way along its length, but it no longer pleased Giles so much.

"I prefer the street empty," he said firmly. He drew the curtains and turned on his reading-lamp. It was his own book he was reading. For ten years now Giles had been writing a history of his own family and Murreinhead. The story began in 1561 with the arrival of Mary Stuart, Queen of Scots, back home from France upon the death of her first husband and ended... but it hadn't yet ended. And sometimes Giles thought his writing of the book would never end either. He had written it once as a straight history book and it had seemed dull even to him. You couldn't get excitement out of it. So now he was writing it as a historical novel. Or more accurately, as a series of historical novels. This too moved slowly: he was still stuck with Mary and her ferocious kinsmen. He re-read what he had written yesterday; it sounded good.

The desk was a little dusty and he absently rubbed at it with his handkerchief Giles lived alone in the old house and looked after himself. The days of kindly motherly old housekeepers are over except for the rich and Giles was poor, sometimes astonishingly poor, and had never anyway liked being mothered. A succession of daily cleaners tried to help. Lizzie had been the very first when he had newly come to the town.

"Took advantage of my ignorance," was how Giles put it.

For what Giles hid as much as possible, hid even from himself and even sometimes forgot, was that there was a gap of some eighty years when no Almond had lived or worked in Murreinhead, and that it had been Giles who had come back here and romantically set up shop.

And jolly ungrateful they were, too, he thought reminiscently. Especially ungrateful had been William Tulloch, who had been happily and prosperously practising law in the town for the last thirty years. He was still prosperous and no longer alarmed. "The man's a dilettante," he had rolled out in description of Giles, giving every consonant full weight. But he had put the business he didn't want in Giles's way and had watched with tolerance Giles's gradual establishment of himself in the town.

Giles worked on, his face in thought, unconsciously adopting that remote dreamy look which, when seen in court, was apt to make Mr Tulloch mutter. "Ach, the Almonds were always funny folk," he told himself often. "You could never be wither or tither with them," he did not remember the Almonds himself, but his old mother had had one or two stories that he was now dredging up from his memory. "Old Jessie Almond once spit in my e'en," was one particularly vivid phrase that he tried to suppress. It *must* be another

Almond. He himself had a very pretty young daughter. "Sir Giles and Lady Almond he had once or twice tried out on his tongue. The possession of a baronetcy had in no way assisted Giles in his attempt to build a business as a lawyer. "Ah, but the lad'll have to be doing a lot better than he is to afford a wife," was Mr Tulloch's summing up.

Giles got up. "I need another book," he tripped delicately down the stairs. You had to be careful on the stairs still, he hadn't got round to restoring the top of the house yet. His ancestral home had been almost derelict when the first Almond for almost eighty years moved back into it. Giles was slowly and carefully restoring it. A good deal he did himself but some expensive re-wiring and re-plumbing had made him a popular figure among the tradesmen of the town. His plumber had invited him to the Burns Night Supper on the strength of his new copper piping alone. However, only the ground floor and the first flight of stairs were really safe yet, and Giles was still camping out in the rest. He had good ideas about his own comfort, though, and lived well in one great room which had once been the drawing-room and now served him as bedroom and study. This lovely oval room with curving walls faced the street and gave him the view he loved. He felt a proprietary interest in this view. Hadn't his great-great-grandfather been responsible for creating it? Financing the actual building of it and working with Mr Adam the architect from Edinburgh? Giles still had an original fireplace in marble and stucco in his beautiful battered drawing room and it was a great comfort to him when he felt sad.

Giles was often sad. He could never account for it; there never seemed any reason for his moods of loneliness and dullness. Perhaps it was wrong to call them sadness; they were more a sort of despair. He envied William Tulloch his steady good spirits.

It never occurred to Giles to associate his moods of depression with malnutrition and his regular diet of coffee, salad and porridge. Or, for that matter, to link Willie Tulloch's cheer with whisky. He *had* noticed that his spirits were lowest round about five-thirty on a Sunday night.

Saturday night, however, was usually a time of happiness (he had fish and chips for supper that night) and he moved down the stairs lightly, even the memory of Lizzie Hamilton's slow gait down the road no longer annoying him. He had always maintained she moved at that deliberate solid pace to annoy people. No one was fast moving in Murreinhead but Lizzie was far and away the slowest. He knew that to a lot of people Lizzie was a sturdy 'character' with a heart of gold. But Giles thought she was deceitful and vain, and he suspected she was unkind to her husband. She had certainly been unkind to him. She had treated him scornfully and without courtesy as soon as she had seen his books and sensed what he was like. In her heart she despised books and book learning and it seemed very suitable to her that Giles was poor. To

Giles she was the prototype of the people who had put iron staircases across the front of some of the street's handsome houses, knocked extra windows in some parts of the facades and put garish shop fronts in others.

Nevertheless, he did not think that Lizzie Hamilton had slashed Mrs Louden's coat. Slashing coats wasn't Lizzie's line at all. Lizzie liked a show of violence as well as anyone, no doubt about that, the variety of bruises sported by Mr Hamilton and the crockery she had broken for Giles bore witness to this side of her. But Lizzie was very very respectable. Beating husbands and smashing crockery was lawful and slashing coats was not. Lizzie liked to be on the side of the law.

Well, we adjourned the case, thought Giles, so the question is still open. The case had been adjourned for one month because Mrs Louden had sent a letter and a doctor's certificate saying she was ill. Giles had heard later that she had been seen walking round the streets looking perfectly healthy. There were invisible illnesses, though.

Giles selected a book from the bookshelves in his office. It was Dugdale's *Baronage*, a strange book to find in the office of a country lawyer, and certainly an extravagant one. It represented several weeks of austere living on Giles's part. His office, although plain, showed another side of Giles's character. No one looking round it could fail to miss that he was a determined and industrious young man. Willie Tulloch was underrating him. All Giles needed was time, and he would cut a figure in Murreinhead. But it would be on his own terms.

During all the time he had lived there he had set up no real relationships, not quarrelled, not fallen in love, but had remained as invulnerable as in a dream. And perhaps this was the true reason for his sadness.

But secure in this invulnerability, aware that all his loyalties were to things, and that he was committed to no one, he was incredulous to find himself suddenly engaged at the heart of a local mystery. Engaged? The word should be embattled. And that's a fine way for a respectable young lawyer to be, he thought grimly.

He believed Mrs Hamilton when she said she had not slashed Robertina Louden's coat. But he believed that on a larger scale she was lying.

He *wanted* to prove Lizzie Hamilton guilty.

Lizzie Hamilton knew how he felt, as well as anybody, and prepared to do battle on her own account.

"He's out for me," she said to her eldest and married daughter.

"Oh, Mum, you shouldn't say that," protested her daughter.

"He doesnae like me and I dinna like him," said Mrs Hamilton. "The wee foreigner."

"Ye canna say that, Mother. It's an old family in the town."

"I never heard tell of it."

"There's Almond Crescent and Almond Place," pointed out her daughter. "But they've been away from the town for eighty years. Now he's come back." She found Giles rather a romantic figure herself.

"Away eighty years and the town's got on fine without them," said Lizzie triumphantly. "And we could have gone on getting on fine," she finished, unconsciously echoing the words of Willie Tulloch.

"Mum!" protested her daughter. She eyed her mother nervously. She wasn't so afraid of her mother as some of the rest of the family. After all, she was a married woman and had a husband to protect her. She had taken care to marry a good strong brawny man. Now she was slightly frightened of him. Lizzie's children were born to be terrified.

"But I never slashed her coat. And I told the court so."

"No, Mum."

"No. And she knows it now."

"*Now*, Mum?" said her daughter questioningly. Her mother said nothing.

Coffin drew the curtains closed against the sun, and turned to his wife. The long summer of unbroken heat still went on. It was Friday, May 29th. He was two weeks older and two weeks hotter. He also had had disquieting news. It looked as though a new pattern was appearing in his district. In the epidemology of crime a pattern was something to be feared.

"Hot, hot, hotter."

"Yes," said his wife.

"Like India. Ought to send you up to the hills or something," he threw up the window. "Still, it's evening now. Nasty day it's been," he was really thinking of himself and his own life.

"I've rather enjoyed it," said his wife, who was thinking of hers. "My day was pleasant. I think the rehearsals are going well. And the clothes are heavenly. It's almost worth appearing in such a bad play just to wear them."

"Is it a bad play?" asked her husband, surprised.

"Terrible. Glib," her tone almost contradicted her assertion that it had been a good day. As Cleopatra Partridge she was a successful actress, but she hadn't acted for over a year now. This was her comeback. For this reason it was very important to her. Her friend Venetia Stuart was the star.

"I thought you liked it."

"I like my part. I like the feel of it in my hand, do you see? But it's a bad play."

Coffin was silent. He would never understand the actor's temperament, he thought. "Still, the clothes are good," he said finally.

"The best I've ever seen. We shall run for months on the decor and dress alone."

"I don't like to think of you acting in something bad and glib."

40

"Oh. Oh."

The street light came through the now uncurtained window and shone on a polished table. One light shone in the corner of the room and a moth fluttered round it.

"Let the silly thing out," said his wife.

He turned off the lamp carefully. "It'll go now." For a moment they sat in darkness.

"Perhaps when the light comes on we shall have different faces," said Patsy suddenly. "Switch it on and let's see. No, you look just the same. What about me?"

"The same. Shall I turn the light out for longer?"

"No. We're too old. When you get past a certain age, you've built up your face, you've built your character round it, you *can't* change, you don't want to."

"You change your face ten times a day, I've seen you."

"Oh, I always change back at night."

They both laughed.

"You know, I don't think those clothes can be so wonderful," said Coffin, studying her face. "You look tired," he did not tell her that Venetia Stuart had telephoned him that Patsy had had an argument with both the producer and the couturier who was making her clothes and what about taking her out to dinner and getting her drunk or something.

"Ah, this is where the plot begins," said his wife. "Someone's writing your lines for you."

"I think it must be a rotten play," said Coffin

41

leaning back and speaking dispassionately. "Empty the theatre."

"That's what's worrying me."

"So that's it," said Coffin, taking her hand. "*You* won't have a failure, *you* won't have a flop."

"I've had them before."

"No, you're just nervous because you haven't been playing for over a year. I tell you I can see the gold glittering on this one."

"I suppose Venetia telephoned and told you I was in a temper."

"Yes, of course," said Coffin, letting go of her hand. "You know Venetia: everyone's little helper."

"Did I tell you that she's bought a diamond and sapphire tiara?" said his wife, looking more cheerful.

"Oh well, there you are, that shows you. Venetia knows the play's going to earn a mint of money."

"Venetia's bought plenty of things she couldn't pay for. Perhaps she's going into one of her bad cycles." Venetia was famous for her extravagances. She had once bought a whole troupe of dancing cats who were otherwise doomed to be put down, and said she was going to do the music halls with them. The six cats lived with her for three months, fighting and screaming and never dancing once. Probably they had forgotten how. Perhaps they had never known. While her cat period lasted Venetia was the most unpopular woman in London, even with dogs. The cats went everywhere with her, some hanging over her arms like fur muffs; others draped round her neck, the rest walking behind calling. It was a circus in itself. At the end of it, Venetia was exhausted and no longer sure if she was cat or human. The cats were then triumphantly bought back at a low price by their former owner who at once tried to sue Venetia for alienation of their affections. And it was true that the cats, with the perversity of their tribe, constantly tried to make their way back to the flat where they had rioted so happily. Venetia nearly emigrated that year.

"It's more a little crown than a tiara, really," added Patsy.

"Even Venetia won't be able to wear a crown too often."

"She was wearing it to the theatre this morning. It looked wonderful too. The trouble with Venetia is that she's never forgotten that way back in 1929 she was once engaged to a Russian Prince for three weeks."

"It was the Grand Dukes that counted, not the Princes," said Coffin. "Anyone could be a Prince."

"So we keep telling her. And of course he wasn't even a real Russian Prince. He went to prison not long afterwards, that was what broke the engagement off."

"I should have thought Venetia would have enjoyed the romance of being engaged to a prisoner."

"Not to a bigamist, she wouldn't."

"I always wonder what Venetia's motives in marrying are, anyway," observed Coffin.

"Oh, she has the usual ones, the same as anyone else," said his wife, a trifle sharply. They were on dangerous ground; both knew it. "She's not immune."

What Patsy was really saying by implication was: she can be a fool like anyone else. She hadn't made a remark like this for months now. Was everything starting up again? They stared at each other uneasily.

"Look after your handbag when you go out shopping, will you?" he said abruptly. "Especially if you go up the Red."

After a lull of two weeks, during which no snatches had been reported, there had been another six episodes that day.

On the next day, there were seven more. All silent, all successful. On each occasion a knife had been used.

On Sunday it stopped again. No more thefts were reported.

On Monday the hot weather faltered for the first time and there was rain. It was also Patsy's dress rehearsal; she looked both radiant and angry.

"We have a disease," said Coffin, studying a list of the incidents. "It's like a recurring fever. We have it and no one else has," he put the papers down on his desk.

"He might move elsewhere," said Dove.

"Tell me what you really think."

"I don't know why we haven't caught him already," said Dove with sudden irritation.

"That's what I think too," said Coffin, bending

over the papers.

The next Friday, the first Friday in June, they set up a decoy: a young policewoman wearing a light cotton dress and dark spectacles, and swinging a white handbag over her arm. Behind the dark spectacles her eyes were alert.

For some time she shopped, gossiped, and strolled in the sun.

But nothing happened to her. No one touched her handbag and no one even came very close.

The next day she was replaced by a more matronly woman, pushing a pram. The pram contained her own baby. She was an ex-policewoman specially recruited for the job.

There was one moment when she stood on the kerb, the baby crying in the pram, and grabbed at a woman passer-by. But it was a false alarm. The decoy's handbag had simply got caught up in the other woman's shopping.

Nevertheless, the two decoys had something to tell Coffin. Each repeated her conviction that no one was 'working' the market while she had been on the alert. They hadn't been lucky or simply avoided by a smart criminal... The market was genuinely 'dead'.

There was another, more puzzling factor, too. The local professionals were not showing anger or resentment at this highly successful invasion of their territory but something between bewilderment and fear. They disassociated themselves sharply from it. It was something different.

"Not like us."

"Fancy."

"Not right."

"Creepy."

These were the words passing round. There was a certain quiet nastiness to the knife which no one liked.

Perhaps it reminded them all of Jack the Ripper.

An unexpressed, inarticulate suspicion grew up that the bag slitting was a simple substitute, a cover over the criminal's real desires that perhaps he dared not lift himself, a symbol for what he *really* wished to do.

A bag is round and soft and at least pretends that it is leather, which was once skin. Within this bag are protected objects of value. The slash had been a long savage slitting tear severing the cords of the bag. Yes, as well as a theft, this action could be a symbol.

"A baby mass murderer," grunted Coffin, catching the thought that was in the wind. "That's what we may be breeding up here."

But, if so, what was it leading up to?

Every four weeks a circular newsletter is unofficially sent round to all heads and assistant heads of detective forces in the United Kingdom. It contains confidential and necessary information of the sort that is better passed on unofficially. Needless to say it is avidly read. The compiler is a retired policeman living in a suburb of Manchester.

As a Divisional Detective Inspector, Coffin got a copy.

Dove drew Coffin's attention to one item it contained.

"Here, take a look at this," he planted the paper in front of Coffin.

"I've seen that. There's nothing in it." Coffin barely looked up.

"Then you haven't looked properly." Dove folded the paper back and pointed. "Here, the bit about the slashed coats."

Coffin picked it up and read the indicated passage. It was a report from the Chief Inspector, Murreinhead, Angus, and it stated that in Murreinhead there had been three cases of coat slashing in three weeks.

"It's not the same," Coffin dismissed it.

"It's like." Dove could be obstinate.

Coffin was studying the item from Murreinhead. "Never anything at the weekend. Always midweek."

"Yes. I saw that. I never said it was identical."

"One case pending. Looks as though they've got the joker."

"I think it's interesting. Worth having a look."

"Perhaps you're right." Coffin was only half convinced. "But what possible connection can there be between us here in London and Murreinhead?"

He stood there, holding the paper, twisting it between his hands as if it could give him the answer. He was watching a motor stop opposite and an elderly man get out.

"The doctors are busy this week, aren't they?" he said idly as he stared out of the window. "I keep seeing them go into fresh houses. What's the sickness of this hot summer?"

Chapter 4

THE BURGH COURT of Murreinhead met, as Giles often had opportunity of observing, in circumstances of great discomfort. The building was an old one, not romantically old, merely inconveniently so. One issue on which Giles and Willie Tulloch spoke harmoniously in tune was that the lavatories were disgraceful. Giles hoped that one day the building would fall down and allow him to get at the foundations. He was sure there was a medieval crypt underneath. Not for nothing did the building stand on a piece of land called Priorsgait. Once or twice he had found himself kicking the walls hopefully; but although they looked rotten, they were sturdy.

Even on this warm day in early June the building smelt damp. Giles sniffed.

"Don't you think that smell is dry rot?" he asked Tulloch hopefully.

Willie did not answer.

"The whole building will fall down around us one day," went on Giles. He went round tapping and rapping on the walls. "Look at that. Bulging with damp. Absolutely riddled with rot. That's what the smell is. The place will collapse."

"No, it won't," said Tulloch. "Smelt like that for the last thirty years and it hasn't collapsed."

"Thirty years," said Giles, aghast. He began to wonder if he would still be here smelling it and complaining in a further thirty years. Probably he would. He wanted to change things, improve them. It wasn't going to be any good at all if buildings and people resisted.

"It's a grand fine building," said Willie Tulloch defiantly.

Giles looked at him standing there, foursquare and sturdy in his bright tweed suit and woollen tie. Yes, if he, Giles, was here in thirty years' time, Willie and the building would certainly make it too.

"They might at least repaint it," was all he said.

"Repaint it! It was done for the Queen's coronation!"

But since that repainting, some years ago now after all, numerous feet had scuffed at the wainscoting and kicked at the doors and several hands had scrawled rude messages on the paler parts of the walls, which scrubbing had only partly removed.

"Ah, we can't be watching them all the time," said Willie, glancing round him tolerantly. Then his eye fell upon a pencilled phrase which clearly said *Tullie got me three months.* "Perhaps we should, though," he ended.

Giles looked sympathetic. Out of the corner of his eye he could see the court was filling up. There were going to be plenty of onlookers this morning. And he knew why: Lizzie Hamilton's case was coming up.

"I know the writing, too," said Willie, brushing his knees and getting up from the floor where he had been studying the pencilled insult. He spoke sadly. "It's young Ian Jimson. I did my utmost for that boy. I really put my heart into it. He seemed worth it at the time. I didn't know then what a deceitful boy he was. Three months indeed. It might have been three years."

"Anyone can see he was a liar just from looking at the writing," said Giles. He glanced down at the wall where Tulloch had been crouching. "Anyone who writes at that level must have something to hide." Their eyes met in understanding; a small spark of genuine friendliness was alight.

Fancy hurting the old boy's feelings like that. Why, he's as good as gold, thought Giles. Aloud he said absently, "Ever been to London, Tulloch?"

"I was through it once. A fair city but dirty. I go to Edinburgh regularly, though. Why?"

"I just wondered." You couldn't say: I'm just seeing you as a person for the first time. I want to start asking questions about you.

Willie clicked his teeth and looked irritated. One of the things that annoyed him most about Giles was the young man's capacity for going off at a tangent. He was unpredictable.

"It's a long expensive trip from here," said Giles. The front two rows of seats were full now of Lizzie's friends. Or were they her enemies?

"Ach, it's not so expensive if you know the right way to go," said Willie. He turned away to greet his daughter who acted as his secretary. She was much prettier than seeing Willie would have led you to expect, in fact she was a beauty.

Giles knew this of course; he had danced with her at several local balls. Unfortunately she didn't like him. Perhaps she felt wary of a young man so clearly dedicated to the restoration of the antiquities of her native town. Beautiful young girls prefer dedications to be present and personal.

Catriona gave Giles her usual remote, even hostile glance, bowed her head slightly and drew her father away. She knew exactly how to behave like a duchess. "A blasted duchess," as Giles put it to himself. It suddenly came to him that one of the questions he ought to ask about Willie was how he came to have this lovely daughter. Perhaps it was Mrs Tulloch. He really ought to meet Mrs Tulloch. But no one ever did meet Mrs Tulloch. She was seen nowhere. Why didn't she go out? Willie got out enough. He might not get to London but you saw him around all the time in his own town. He was at every luncheon party, every tea party, carrying his white gloves. Every Sunday he went to Kirk in his top hat, one of the last five left in Murreinhead. Giles reflected that he looked extremely handsome in his top hat, so perhaps Catriona got her looks from Willie after all.

Catriona was bending over her books and papers, competently arranging her father's work. Catriona was clever, and there was no doubt at all about where she got her brains: her father.

A faint pinkness crept up the girl's throat and on to her cheeks. Giles did not connect it with his presence or his gaze.

He looked up and saw that the Magistrate had arrived. It was Daniel Blair today. But there seemed to be a stir and bustle at the door and he saw James McGinn pushing in behind. Giles frowned. There was really no call for the presence of Mr McGinn.

Daniel Blair sat down at the Magistrates' table and James McGinn tucked himself in beside him; he was a tiny neat man who looked smaller than ever beside Big Daniel. (There was a Little Daniel in the town, a joiner.)

"I'm ready, Mr Clerk," said Blair. "Ready," he always addressed Giles in this manner. Eccentric, Giles had thought at first, but was now used to it. He was used also to the impatience, the faint hint of the whip. People said that old Blair had been a first-class headmaster before he gave up scholasticism to run the family business, but somehow one felt that discipline and not instruction had been his forte.

The courtroom was a square high-ceilinged room and the Magistrates sat on a small platform hardly dignified enough to be called a dais. Giles had a desk to the right and a third desk stretched to the left. The public had plain wooden seats facing the Magistrates. The whole effect was quiet and rather domestic. In the beginning it had seemed to Giles that it gave no hint of the ancient authority of Scots Law which lay behind it. He had started out full of romantic respect for the sturdy body of law he was to practise, law created out of the history and customs of the Lowland Scot, acknowledging

English law but not necessarily receiving it, and it had seemed to him that the proceeding in Murreinhead's Burgh Court did not take itself as seriously as he did. The constant pauses for consideration, the prolonged discussions of small detail, the ready adjournments seemed to him fussy. But slowly he came to see it all as marking a deep respect for law; and since taking over as Clerk to the Court, he had contributed himself to the discussions and delay.

He did so now.

"One minute, please," he bent his head over his papers: yes, the Knowles case was to be presented first, rather out of turn, at the express wish of Sergeant Santonelli of the Murreinhead Police Force, who had said with feeling, that if Agnes Dyke humiliated him any more then he had to have the rest of the day to get over it.

"Alexander James Knowles against Agnes Dyke," he announced, but not very loudly, almost to himself. "Eh?" said Mr Blair.

"Alexander James Knowles," began Giles.

"Yes. Yes. I know," he looked about the court and then said in a loud bright voice, well audible and meant to be so: "That's the lady with the ghosts, isn't it?"

"They were mentioned." Giles could see a blush spreading across Sergeant Santonelli's face. He had not enjoyed his experience with Agnes Dyke's ghosts. The poor sergeant, he thought. He had often been considerably exasperated himself by Miss

54

Dyke. He could see her now in court, alert with anger and quite ready to speak up for herself. It might have been that parrot of hers, he said to himself I can't believe in those ghosts.

"The case, the case, Mr Clerk," said the Bench irritably. "It is now nearly eleven o'clock. Shall we begin?"

"Agnes Dyke, at the instance of the complainant, Alexander James Knowles, you are accused of having trespassed on the property of said Alexander James Knowles, to wit his hen-run and to have defaced and knocked down said hen-run. How do you plead?"

"Not guilty," said Agnes Dyke stoutly, standing and speaking in a loud voice. "For I didna, and I said so before."

"That's enough," said Mr Blair. Agnes Dyke sold him his finnan haddie and his smokies every week for his breakfast and his salmon twice a month when in season. He knew her well.

"Nor did I burn it down," continued Agnes irrepressibly.

"And I never said you did," said Alexander Knowles, getting up and speaking in his turn; he too spoke over loudly.

"There's those who say it."

They faced each other angrily.

Not much hope of peace there, thought Giles, *they* won't come to terms. Why ever did we bother to adjourn the case? Why did we ever hear it? Why didn't they fight it out in the first place? However, since this consummation could not be allowed in *plein cour* he cleared his throat and spoke sternly.

"Silence, please." I sound like something out of Lewis Carroll, he thought.

"Sergeant Santonelli, will you come forward, please?"

Santonelli was a strange name to find in Scotland. George Santonelli was a member of a family which had come to Scotland from Naples over ninety years ago to open a shop, had prospered and stayed. Their cousins, the Fraticellis, had followed them out, and *their* cousins the Buonos. The Santonellis were now a respected part of Murreinhead society. They had not forgotten their origin and once a year one or other of them went back to the family village of Anchiano, but they were British citizens and felt no doubt about it. George Santonelli, now thirty, had served three years in the Black Watch. "Our George is not clever, he must do something practical," was how the Santonelli clan put it, but George in fact was quite clever in his way and made a good police officer. He was very interested in doorways (there were lots of fine doorways in Murreinhead) and he and Giles had many conversations about them and sometimes went round photographing them.

Santonelli was already moving forward. Agnes Dyke was making a little clucking noise under her breath, thus indicating that she repudiated what was now about to be said, and disassociated herself from it. Santonelli heard the noise and changed from pink to white. He was a sensitive man and felt that he was being discredited. Agnes had once chased him as a boy and his old dog from her back garden for stealing apples; this was twenty-two years ago but it still shaped their relationship.

"On the afternoon of April 22nd," began Santonelli.

"A Wednesday," said Agnes. "I ask you to notice it was a Wednesday."

She was ignored. "I went to No. 14 Creeona Crescent after a series of telephone calls from the complainant, stating that Miss Dyke, his neighbour, was committing repeated and violent trespass on his property."

"She was for chopping down my garden shed where I keep my little hens," said Alexander Knowles. "You shan't be the only one that shouts."

Santonelli ignored him too. "When I got there I found both parties engaged in a fight."

The bruise was fading round Alexander Knowles's left eye, but you could still see it. But for all that it was Alexander who looked triumphant. Agnes was still wearing her hat, and he and he alone knew that underneath it was a wig, and that the wig had come off in the fight.

"They were engaged once, you know," whispered the magistrate to Giles. "It explains a lot."

"Miss Dyke alleged that she had come into Mr Knowles's garden armed with a hatchet, not for the purpose of chopping down his garden shed, but to release her parrot that was caught in her

57

apple tree but which she had to approach from his side. She maintained she was only climbing up the side of his shed for the purpose of getting nearer the bird. While she was saying this she dealt Mr Knowles a blow on the side of the face and said she had a perfect right to come into his garden if she wanted and he knew it. They then started fighting again." The sergeant paused. In the attempt to separate them he had sprained his ankle badly and Agnes Dyke and Alexander Knowles had had to let him limp between them back to the police station. The street had turned out to watch. It had been very humiliating.

The quarrel between the two of them had been going on for such a long time now that no one knew the beginning of it. Alexander's present claim brought to court for the first time a fight that had a long history. Agnes attacking his shed with an axe, if she *had* attacked it, was today's manifestation. Tomorrow there would be something else. It was almost impossible to tell who was telling the truth about what. But one thing was clear: nothing was ever quite what it seemed. Agnes had not been looking for her parrot, Alexander had not attacked her in a rage because she was banging away with a little axe at his shed, and Sergeant Santonelli had not fallen down by accident. No, he had been pushed by one or other of them, and he didn't know which.

"Later that evening," went on the sergeant, "the fire brigade was called to 14 Creeona Crescent because the shed was on fire."

"What a carry on that was," murmured Agnes.

"But the shed was not destroyed?" inquired Mr Blair.

"The fire was put out without much difficulty," said Sergeant Santonelli. "The shed remains."

"Thank you, Sergeant." Santonelli sat down.

"I don't believe it was a *real* fire, said Agnes in a most audible voice.

Like your ghosts, thought Santonelli, meeting the gaze of Giles Almond. The ghosts had just crept into the case. Agnes Dyke had mentioned them when the case first came to court. The attics of her house were ghost-ridden, she complained. She suggested that the magistrate come and listen.

Perhaps she really did have ghosts. Or perhaps she was a little crazy. Or maybe she just wanted people to think she was. But he didn't think so. He thought she had something else in her wicked old mind.

"And let me see, why did we adjourn the case?" asked the magistrate of Giles Almond.

"Because a witness presented himself. Edward Walker who wrote to us saying he had been standing on a ladder and had seen the whole thing."

"And Edward Walker is now here?" asked Mr Blair, looking round him expectantly.

"He is."

Agnes started to click her teeth disparagingly as Edward Walker appeared. She had reason to display her scepticism of Edward Walker well in advance.

"I am Edward Walker and I reside at 3 Hemming's Close. I am a window cleaner." The evidence started mildly.

Edward Walker was a small stocky man with a red face and a soft voice. So soft it was not easy to hear what he said. His little hands moved restlessly while he spoke. Still, he had volunteered his evidence, so he must have wanted to give it.

"I was cleaning the window at Mrs Mackie's, number 12, the house next to Alex Knowles. I was on my ladder, not thinking anything about anything, and I saw Agnes Dyke come out into her garden with her parrot."

The court was silent, listening. Even Lizzie Hamilton at the back of the court, with all she had on her mind, was listening.

"And she climbed over the fence into Alex's. I ken her well, you understand? And she put her parrot in the tree and then she turned to bang at the shed with an axe. The parrot couldn't fly, you see, poor old bird, any more than old Agnes can, so it was quite safe."

"Are you sure you saw all this, Mr Walker?"

"As sure as I'm standing here. She was banging away like mad," said the window cleaner gleefully. "I'm thinking she *wanted* to be heard."

"Ask him what he last went to prison for," called Agnes. "Go on, ask him that."

"Wait a minute," said Mr Blair; he looked stern and cross as he summoned Giles. "What's all this about?" he asked in a low voice. "Is it true? Is she

60

just seeking to discredit the witness?" and here he cast a bleak look towards Agnes Dyke now leaning comfortably back in her chair. "Is he a liar or is she?" He shook his head despairingly. "No, that's a stupid question. I know what Aggie is."

"He *has* been to prison, I believe," murmured Giles.

"We must get the rights of it. Explain to the sergeant," he rapped on the table. "This case is adjourned for one further month."

The day was proceeding, not according to plan; it rocked rather than marched forward. This was often its gait. Giles would have to put up with it. From earliest times it had been the practice to allow evidence of bad reputation to discredit a witness's testimony. Agnes knew all the tricks.

Giles raised his hand in a slight gesture to Santonelli, meant to indicate that they would have to have a talk together. But to his surprise Santonelli hung on in the court. As far as he knew, Santonelli was not concerned with any of the later cases. Neither by nature nor necessity was George Santonelli a spectator; if he was still here then he was here on business.

Presently Giles saw Santonelli coming over towards him.

"Been to London lately?"

"No." Giles was surprised. "Why?"

"Oh, just asking." Idly Santonelli picked up a pencil from Giles's table and rolled it between his fingers. "I've never been there myself. Glasgow's my metropolis."

"I can see it might be." And he could indeed. He could see Santonelli ranging free in the city.

So *that* was where he disappeared to once or twice a year.

"But you get a picture in your mind. Perhaps it's just two word. *Crowded streets.* That was mine. Crowded streets. Those were the words I got."

"Just what we don't have in Murreinhead."

"That's it. So I thought that's where *their* sort of crime comes from. Different from us here. And now we're getting a similar pattern," he sounded excited.

"You won't get a medal."

"And they're asking for all information. It's the coat slashing. Lizzie Hamilton."

Giles saw that he was immensely pleased with his news. He himself wanted to forget London where he had once lived and been poor and unhappy. And much more besides. He was frightened and distrustful of the memories that he had dammed up. But he had an uneasy feeling that the logjam was breaking.

Standing there, with the sensation of the logs rolling and twisting in the rushing water, he heard Santonelli say: "London policeman called Coffin."

I will not know a London policeman called Coffin, he thought defiantly.

"They want all the information we can give them," continued Santonelli happily. "So can I have a complete transcript?"

Giles made a demurring noise.

"Oh well, it doesn't matter. I have a tape-recorder going."

"You can't do that."

"Dan Blair says I can."

"Dan Blair will get his skirts pulled. I'm the lawyer and I say you can't." All the authority of the common law was behind him.

Santonelli looked amused. "I've done it before. On the quiet."

"I'll *tell* you what you want to know afterwards. And there will be a record." Giles was on his dignity. He didn't quite believe Santonelli about the tape-recorder. Santonelli was a careful prudent man who liked the rules kept. But at the same time he liked to arrange things for himself.

"Next case, Mr Clerk," said the magistrate. He had been having a conversation with his companion James McGinn.

The next case was a police prosecution for dangerous driving on a bad hill just outside Murreinhead. The name of the defendant was unknown to Giles and he was surprised to see a pale tense boy of about eighteen stand up.

"Peter Robert Bell, how do you plead?"

"Not guilty." But the voice was so low that Giles had to ask him to repeat it. "Not guilty."

He could hear a stir on the bench behind him and the sound of James McGinn coughing.

The police case was quite clear and Giles carried all the details in his mind. Moreover, he remembered

63

reading at least two accounts of the accident in the newspapers. A car had hit a van on the slope of the hill and dragged this van into a ditch. Two witnesses said the car had been swinging from side to side of the road before it crashed. It had also been going very fast. The witnesses had watched helplessly while the two vehicles collided and rolled into the ditch. Three people had been killed, one had lost his sight and a girl had had three fingers severed from her left hand. The driver of the offending car had escaped almost unhurt.

Now he knew why James McGinn was in attendance. One of the girls, the maimed one, had been the child of his friend and partner. She was the only one in the incident who came from Murreinhead. All the other people, including the two men in the van, had been outsiders. Peter Bell who was now before the court came from Glasgow.

"I lost control of the car," he said in a husky voice. "I remember it sort of dragging away from me as we went down the hill... I don't remember any more."

"Do you propose to call witnesses?" Daniel Blair asked from the Magistrates' table.

Willie Tulloch was acting for the police. "Yes," he sounded surprised.

"Then I should prefer to get on to them first." Daniel Blair was always decisive and knew his own mind. He was a good lawyer for an amateur and shrewd about medical evidence. Giles respected him. But he had his foibles. And one of them was

64

that he liked to lead into the evidence gradually. He liked to lay the foundations first. He often came to a clash with Willie Tulloch, who preferred to bang away with his big guns like an artillery bombardment. "Haig was a grand soldier," he was accustomed to say with admiration; and he conducted his cases like a battle of the First World War.

James McGinn said nothing, but stared at the defendant, who gazed sadly forward into space as if nothing could ever touch him deeply again.

Inside the court there was the usual slight noise made up of small body movements, subdued coughs and whispers. Outside, there was the occasional sound of a lorry or a bus. Today, because it was so hot, the windows were open. The belt of heat stretched from London to beyond Murreinhead, bringing with it sharpened tempers and odd depressions. Little illnesses afflicted people, summer colds, recalcitrant coughs, irritable rashes, due, the doctors said, to the heat. In addition, Murreinhead suffered from a summer sickness carried perhaps by the insects, which were numerous that year. Or perhaps it came from the ships that docked in Murreinheadport, the town on the sea that was so much bigger and more flourishing than Murreinhead itself. A few sailors always found their way back into Murreinhead. Three colliers a month left Murreinheadport for London, loaded with coal from the declining pits of the district; these were the last remnants of a once proud trade that had brought the 'coalmen' in force to nineteenth-century London.

Giles arbitrated tactfully in the argument developing between the Magistrate and Willie Tulloch, to the fury of both of them. It was in ways like this that Giles betrayed that in everything but ancestry he was a stranger to Murreinhead.

The two witnesses were called and deposed, what everyone already knew, that they had seen the car swerve and then crash into the van. The second witness was an echo of the first.

"It was going fast?"

"Yes. Very fast. Yes, I am a driver myself and I think I am able to estimate speed. I think it was going somewhere between seventy and eighty. No, I had a good view. From where we stood you can see the curve of the road right down the hill. Yes, I saw the driver of the car clearly. I see him now. I helped drag the bodies clear of the wreck. No, I did not call the police. Someone else did that."

The boy wasn't defending himself. He had a solicitor from Glasgow with him but there was no spirit in either of them. They seemed to have made up their minds in advance to be condemned. The spiritless docile quality about them irritated Giles. A man ought to defend himself, was what he thought.

Daniel Blair intervened from the bench.

"You say you did not report the accident to the police? Your companion who gave evidence first says the same thing. Who did report this accident to the police?"

He looked around the room waiting for an answer. Willie Tulloch consulted his papers and whispered with Catriona.

"The police received a telephone call."

"From whom?"

Willie, slightly fussed, once more read through his notes. The court waited.

"It was never discovered," he said finally and with reluctance. "The call was anonymous and was never traced. It was a local call."

"Naturally." Daniel Blair looked thoughtful. "I will adjourn the case," he said. "I would like to consult with the police."

The Burgh Court of Murreinhead took itself seriously. It was at the very bottom of the judicial hierarchy; it decided no important cases, civil or criminal: these went before the Sheriff's Court. But many causes had their first airing at the Burgh Court. It was a court of summary jurisdiction but it was independent and had great powers of investigation. In Murreinhead these powers and this independence were exploited to the full.

Two more cases were dealt with rapidly before lunch. Lizzie Hamilton and her supporters departed in a group to eat.

"Ah, they're away to Rag's Tavern to eat. Old man Rag is Lizzie's cousin and he'll make it a cheap meal for them provided they eat together and eat what he gives them." "What's behind this coat slashing business, do you know?"

"Ach, just a woman's quarrel," said Willie.

"Well, but Santonelli says..." Giles stopped. He would not discuss what Santonelli had said now. "There have been other cases, you know. Three others."

"But no charges have been made. These things are infectious, perhaps. A form of hysteria. The heat," he looked sadly up at the grey sullen sky. "Aye, we might be in the tropics." Perhaps to Willie in his good grey tweed it did indeed feel a tropical heat.

Giles shook his head. "I don't think so."

"Of course. She's a deep woman, Lizzie Hamilton. Very deep."

In London the heat was stronger and the skies lower. The demolition of Creevey Buildings, due to begin this week had been postponed. A quick look at the structure had persuaded the engineers that the Bastille had probably fallen more easily than this fortress would. The great building still stood unslighted.

The secret inhabitants had changed. They were always changing. As some moved out other lost wanderers moved in. The same formalities of non-recognition were observed. No one ever saw or heard anyone else. The dust and refuse mounted on the stairways and grew smelly in the hot sun.

The dog found all this interesting and even exciting. The wound on his leg had healed and he no longer limped, or only when tired. He was living regularly on the second floor now. The atmosphere of odorous decay just suited him. Besides, his friend came there. His friend and once the friend's friend, if the latter *was* a friend. Certain things aroused doubts.

They had not come together.

But they had greeted each other in what he recognised to be familiar terms.

Then the friends had shouted at each other.

These were puzzling aspects, things which at once united and yet separated them in the dog's mind.

But about them both had hung the same smells. His was not a mind which dealt readily in categories but he had recognised a relationship between them which not everyone had seen.

The doctors continued to be busy in this part of London. Coffin himself suffered.

He was an abominable patient.

"Only a really great man ought to be as bad a patient as you are," said his wife, as she stood by his bedside. She had got herself up efficiently as a nurse in a white apron and with her long hair pinned back. She looked pretty and well. She seemed to improve in life and spirits accordingly as her husband went down. It was always the same with them. One of the difficulties about their marriage was that they never both seemed to be on one plane at the same time.

"What's that?" growled her husband. In times

of illness he was inclined to be sure he was a great man, an unappreciated great man and one just about to die at that. When he was better he shrank back to life-size

"You're only pseudo-great," said his wife, sitting by his side on the bed and putting her feet up.

"What do you mean?" He was still suspicious.

"Goodness, my feet ache. Nursing you and doing a matinee is no joke." It was well past midnight but Patsy was gay and ready for another performance. "Well, what was it you are supposed to have had? Didn't the doctor say?"

"He couldn't give it a name," said the patient proudly. "But he said that although there's a lot of sickness around just now, I'm the first case like me he's met."

Patsy started to laugh. The differences between them melted. They were united in self-mockery.

Coffin was one of the first cases of this sort of sickness in his manor. It was a short vicious bout of fever and nausea. The doctors found it puzzling.

Every court day in Murreinhead a lunch party, not entirely congenial in all its elements, assembled in the Rayburn Arms. The Rayburn was an austere but beautiful eighteenth-century building about whose restoration Giles was determined soon to set. Every time he went into the building his fingers itched to tear down the false partitions, papered in fading red wallpaper, which masked the beauty of

70

the oval hall. Why should the noble proportions be obscured by the gentlemen's cloakroom?

Giles went over and looked at the curving mahogany staircase and gave it a friendly stroke. Willie Tulloch, observing him, looked shocked, as though Giles had done something improper. And yet Willie himself, as Giles had often observed with baffled irritation, had instinctive good taste. It was true he lived in his handsome stone house amid the Edwardian upholstery selected by his mother as a bride, but when he himself chose anything new it was always strikingly in keeping with the real date of the house. There was a breakfronted bookcase and a late eighteenth-century estate desk which Giles coveted. And Catriona herself dressed beautifully. It couldn't all come from nowhere.

"Nice thing," he said to Willie. "I like houses."

"I've noticed."

They went up the stairs into the dining room, whose windows overlooked the main street with much the same view as Giles's house. Their usual table by the window was ready, with Daniel Blair already seated and supping his soup. It was an informal arrangement but it suited them all. Giles, at first horrified, now found it cosy and comfortable. Also the food was good and Giles was greedy. He looked round hungrily now and said, "Scotch broth, please," to the waitress.

Catriona was eating grapefruit and looking severe. She did not smile at Giles. Some days she did, some days she didn't. Today was obviously an

71

off day. He never knew what pleased her. Or, for that matter, displeased her. But he had a deep urge to bring a smile to that long beautiful face.

"Good morning. Miss Tulloch," he had never yet summoned up courage, to call her Catriona. It would have been unasked in any case.

"Good morning, Sir Giles." She too was always equally formal; there was even the slight suggestion of a bow as she spoke.

"Will you be at the Liberal Ball, Miss Catriona?" He was rather pleased with himself for thinking suddenly of this formula which sounded elective if antique. It certainly marked a step forward.

"I shall not." Catriona went on with her grapefruit. Too late, he remembered that Willie was a Unionist and Catriona, whatever her private politics (and frankly from the look he had sometimes seen cross her face, he thought they might be pretty radical) would not let her father down in public.

"I'm not going myself."

"You'd need a new set of tails if you did," observed Catriona, finishing her grapefruit.

Giles was surprised. His suit was certainly old, he believed it had at one time belonged to his grandfather, but the cloth was splendid.

"The cut is so very antique. You are more fond of dressing up houses than yourself, Giles," said Catriona kindly.

Giles was so hurt that he did not notice for some time that he had at last advanced on to less formal terms with Catriona. He was Giles.

"Omelette," Catriona said to the waitress.

Daniel Blair spoke across the table. "You're not eating, I see, Catriona."

"I've had a grapefruit," she said, surprised.

"Grapefruit's no food," he did not really approve of Catriona's presence there. In the old days the luncheon had been a purely masculine occasion. A chance, as Daniel said, to have a crack with an old friend. How could you have a crack with an old friend while a young girl looked at you with bright clever eyes, and probably remembered all you said to your disadvantage? He was always a little uneasy in women's company. Like Giles, he had no doubts about the quality of Catriona's intelligence.

"Catriona minds her figure," said her father.

"I like grapefruit," said Catriona, and Giles decided that to beauty and brains Catriona added obstinacy. She was certainly a formidable girl.

Giles drank his soup, ate venison with red currant jelly, and finished with trifle, eating it defiantly while Catriona austerely sipped black coffee.

As lunch finished, Daniel Blair moved over and started a low-voiced conversation with his friend Willie Tulloch. Giles thought that judging by his expression Willie was bored by it and would really have preferred to take his usual light nap. "Oh, aye," he said at intervals. "Oh, aye." After a while he lit a cigar and puffed away at it, his face expressionless.

Catriona watched them.

"Will Daniel get what he is after?" asked Giles in

a whisper.

"Is he after something?" Catriona was giving nothing away.

"You know he is. It's written all over him. He wants something from your father."

"Perhaps."

"I wish I knew what it was." There were one or two local problems hanging fire at the moment and Daniel's long serious plea to his friend might concern any one of them. Daniel might be discussing the new school playground, which was badly needed. It was a strange thing about that playground; it was small and badly drained and sunless, but they had had two deputations from the children (one of boys, one of girls, Murreinhead believed in the segregation of the sexes) each to ask if their old playground could be saved. Saved was the word they used—as if it was a treasure to be preserved. That was one problem. Or it might be Daniel was talking about the restoration of the medieval priory building down by the river and long in use as a pig shed. This rebuilding was dear to Giles's heart but not to the ratepayers who would be asked to pay for it, and Daniel was an important ratepayer. Then there was the question of whether or not to take up the cobbles in the High Street and replace them with paving stones. Giles, the antiquarian, was in favour of leaving them, while Daniel, the shop-owner, was not. All of these problems could be under discussion now.

He saw Daniel rap his hand on the table once or twice.

74

"He's pushing things a bit," he said judicially. "He must be keen to get his way."

"Then he won't get it," said Catriona with sudden impatience. She stood up. "Two o'clock, Father."

Willie looked at her dreamily and Giles wondered if he hadn't perhaps dropped asleep like a horse, with his eyes open.

"Coming, Catriona. See you in court, Dan," he heaved himself up and followed his daughter. "I'm against the car park though. Remember that. I'm against the car park."

Daniel did not look too displeased, however, and made a note in his little brown book that went everywhere with him.

"I don't know that I'm in favour of a car park myself," he said. "But I had to put it to him in the most favourable light. It was my duty. But I won't say I'm displeased to have him come down so strong against it."

"I hadn't even heard about a car park."

"Oh, we don't tell you everything, Sir Giles," said Daniel Blair with a laugh. "No, indeed we don't. Besides, it would make it terribly noisy down your end of the town. You wouldn't want it, you know, you wouldn't want it."

"Who does want it?" asked Giles bluntly.

"One thing hangs upon another, Sir Giles," said Daniel, perfectly good-humoured. He was always good-humoured on court days. He enjoyed them.

"I'm thinking of forming a Society for the Preservation of Murreinhead," said Giles, who could begin to see some remote and terrible threat in the car park.

"Are you, Sir Giles?" answered Daniel as he departed. "I rather thought you were one in yourself." He was laughing as he left. "Always remember I'm interested in *new* Murreinhead," he called back as he went down the stairs.

Giles was the last of the party to leave; by this time he was almost alone in the room except for two girls sitting in the corner eating ice cream. People lunched early in Murreinhead. The large rectangular room with the lofty ceiling and the balcony had been the ballroom of the Rayburn Arms in the days of his ancestors. There was a tradition that beneath the white moulded ceiling one could see an even earlier painted ceiling. Angelica Kauffmann perhaps? Had she ever worked in Scotland? Giles had the ambition of pulling down the Victorian plasterwork one day and having a look. He walked out of the room with his head turned up staring at the ceiling, trying to imagine the classical deities who might be disporting themselves with such angelic good taste and elegance behind it. But today this game lacked its usual flavour. He remembered some of the things he had learnt about his hometown. The gentle, steady under-employment that forced older men often to stand at the street corner by the Labour Exchange and young ones to pack up and leave home. Perhaps the very quietness of life here reflected lack of opportunity. The gilt began to fade from his dream of restoring Murreinhead to what it had been. Perhaps Daniel Blair was right to be on the side of new Murreinhead.

The court resumed its session. The first two cases were simple and easily dealt with. Gradually Giles became aware of the expectancy in the room. Lizzie Hamilton and her party of friends (but were they friends or just wary onlookers?) had been there all day. and soon it would be their turn for the stage. Lizzie anyway made no bones about wanting to play her part well. She had curled her hair, she was wearing make-up and perhaps she had even learned her lines by heart.

It was some time before Giles realised that only one protagonist was there.

Robertina Louden had not yet appeared. He glanced at the clock. It was full time for her to appear. He was keeping his eyes on the door at the back of the court all the time he was helping to dispatch the next piece of business.

"I will make a note of that suggestion, Mr Magistrate, and pass it on; to the Housing Officer." A boy had come quietly into the court and now stood looking round, hesitant and rather nervous. Perhaps Giles's voice faltered, for he saw Daniel Blair give him a sharp look.

"Now," he cleared his throat. "Elizabeth Hamilton against Robertina Louden."

Mrs Hamilton at once stood up.

"I'm Elizabeth Hamilton."

"Mrs Robertina Louden." Giles's gaze was roving round the court. No, Mrs Louden was not present. He raised his voice and spoke loudly, as if he could call out and summon her. He saw the Magistrate look slightly annoyed. "Mrs Louden."

The boy who had just come in stood up.

"She's sick," he called out. He stuttered slightly.

"What?"

"She's sick."

"Did she send another medical certificate?" Mrs Louden had sent one earlier. The boy's face looked blank. "Your doctor…" Giles began.

"Rina's ill," he called her Rina. Not Mother. Yet she must be his mother.

"Your mother?"

"Yes, my mother."

"Well, she ought… your doctor," started Giles once more.

"She's sick," repeated the boy in his hoarse voice. There was a bruise on his face, shaped like a bunch of grapes.

Once again the case was adjourned. But in the interval that necessarily ensued, and while Daniel Blair could be heard making fussy and slightly irritable remarks about delays, Giles went across and spoke to the boy.

"Where do you come from? You're not a local boy?"

"We've moved here, Mum and me," he did not seem inclined to amplify this statement with more

78

detail, but from his accent Giles thought he came from Glasgow.

"Where do you stay?"

"We've got a house down at Hogie's Lane."

"I see." Giles knew those houses. In one way he rather admired them. They were pretty little stone cottages with long country-like gardens. But he thought they were hardly ideal places in which to live, with only one tap and no indoor sanitation. "I thought they were due for demolition," he said absently.

"Ay. But no' yet." The boy scowled. "As soon as you get a place they're all for knocking it down. It's no' fair."

"How did you get that bruise?" Giles had not meant to put the question but it was out now.

The boy touched his hand to his face. "My pals give it to me."

"You've fine friends."

The boy was silent but they stared at each other. A young, torn, violent face looking at Giles's thoughtful one.

"If anyone's been hurting you, you'd better tell me," he knew that bruise had not come from a boys' fight.

"No one's been hurting me," he gave a defiant swing to his body and walked away.

Afterwards Giles spoke to Willie Tulloch.

"I'm almost sure someone's been beating that boy." Whether Willie liked it or not, he was Giles's confidant: he *had* no one else.

79

"I was beaten often enough myself as a boy," said Willie.

"Were you beaten so that you were bruised right down to the bone? For I'm sure he was." Willie frowned; he adopted a business-like approach to life, but underneath he was a sweet-tempered kind man. "There's nothing to be done," he disliked problems where action was impossible.

"We can watch." Watching was to Giles what action was to Willie—his instinctive course of behaviour. You watched, noticed, and presently you could draw a conclusion or pass a judgement. You might not get anything done but at least you *knew*.

That evening Giles went down to Hogie's Lane and stood facing number ten where the Loudens stayed. It was not yet dark; the long Scottish day was only just drawing into dusk. Nevertheless the house looked shut up and still as if everyone was in bed.

Perhaps Rina Louden was ill.

Giles watched for a moment and then walked on.

In the house someone edged quietly away from the window. Presently the front door opened, a figure slipped out and followed Giles almost to his own door where it stood looking up at his window and staring in. Was the figure male or female? In the dark coming down so quickly now it was not possible to see. Huddled in an old coat, head bent, feet dragging but quiet, it seemed to partake of both sexes. Unknown to Giles the watcher and the watched had changed places.

Prescience, the power of self-preservation, common sense, call it what you will, had never been strong in Giles. He had almost lost his life once in London. It might happen the same way any day again.

Chapter 5

THE LITTLE HOUSE in Hogie's Lane where Robertina Louden, Rina, lived with her son Joseph was not as quiet and shut up on the inside as it had seemed to Giles on the outside. Inside a transistor was playing all the time, so that the noise of music spilled very quietly all over the house. This music never stopped except for a short time at night when the radio stations closed down. But this lull only lasted from three o'clock until five-thirty in the morning. Even while Joseph slept voices and music rolled out around him. He had the machine very low indeed but he never turned it off, and lay with his head close to the little box as if wanting company but unwilling to admit it. He *was* unwilling to admit it.

"I'm perfectly all right, thank you. Rina," he said in a loud voice, although he was well aware that Rina could not hear him. "Mother," he said defiantly. He preferred to call her Mother, it seemed to come naturally to his tongue, and oddly enough it suited her, it was how he thought of her. Mother. But Rina said he must call her Rina, that the last thing she wanted was a great boy calling Mother after her down the street.

"I should never have had you," was a variation of this speech, during which she usually stared into Joseph's face as if trying to recognise herself in it. "Or at least not so soon. Ten years later would have been time enough. I was only a kid myself. Rina

82

now, mind, not Mother. I'm not anyone's mother."

So the result was that a new sort of figure was created, Rina-Mother in whom Joseph didn't quite believe and whom he couldn't identify for sure. The person he thought of as Rina wasn't the same person as the one whom he had called Mother and neither had much to do with the person he saw every day. Rina never noticed, never cared, wouldn't have minded that she had practically orphaned him. More, had almost destroyed Joseph himself.

"If I'd been born ten years later I wouldn't have been me," he muttered. "I mean, time matters. It's bound to matter."

He lay on his back in bed and watched the sun rise and lighten the wall of his tiny room and listened to the music begin again on the radio. It was very low so that Rina would not hear, although he knew she would not be disturbed, but it was only an inch from his ear so that the sound flowed into him and poured through him and out again as if he was creating it out of his own breathing, his own vibrating body.

"Dad's coming," he rolled over and away from the music. "Dad's coming today."

Immediately he was sorry he had spoken. Seeing Dad today was not likely to be an enjoyable business. "Wish I hadn't mentioned it," he said regretfully, turning right over and burying his face in the pillow, which smelt of his hair and had done for weeks. "Perhaps I've got the date wrong." But the radio soon set him clear on this. "This is Wednesday, June the tenth," it announced. "Welcome to your early morning programme."

He rolled back again and stared at the ceiling.

"I suppose he could get me into trouble. Take me to court or something... But he wouldn't do that to his own son." There was something in being the son of a father which seemed more enduring than being the son of a mother. That was the view seen from his side; it remained to be seen how Dadhood looked from where his father stood or what weight he would put on the tie. So far, from all Joe had seen in his sixteen years, he had not put much. But a father who was with you for a day or two once or twice a month was hardly working on a full-time basis. No doubt Rina had plenty to make her what she was. But then it could be the other way round—and Rina's character could have produced his itinerant Dad.

Joseph rolled over on his stomach.

"I could hide and pretend that I'm not home when Dad comes." But this was not a good suggestion, and he knew it. Dad would come in, bursting open the door if necessary. Force, not brains, was Dad's weapon. And Joseph did not despise it. By no means.

In court yesterday, he had come near to despising what he saw there.

Rina's right, he had thought. "You can get round 'em. Pull the wool over their eyes."

But it had been unexpectedly hard for him to

stand up there and mutter his excuses about his mother. From the back of the court where he sat it looked like a classroom filled with aged schoolchildren all come to hear the headmaster grumble at them. Perhaps in a little while the master would point at him and he would have to stand up and say the eight times table. Eight it would have to be because this was the one he did not know. He fidgeted in his seat, overcome with all the tensions and irritation of the body that had always attended him in the back row. He was a natural inhabitant of the back row. Any back row.

By the time he had stood up and presented the lame little excuse about Rina, he most energetically regretted that Rina had ever accused Lizzie Hamilton of slashing her coat. And so no doubt, by this time, did Rina.

"I should have stayed right out of the way and not gone there at all." Joe told himself. "I was unwise there. Rina said it's best to always act as if you are telling the truth, but Rina's wrong." One more nail in Rina's coffin, and for him lately there had been plenty of nails. Her extravagance, her meanness, her proximity (they saw far too much of each other) and her positive denial of his right to grow up. Or even, he sometimes thought, her hope that he might cease to exist at all. Rina of course was not a killer. Just a quiet allow-to-die girl. "Rina's wrong… The best thing is to say nothing at all. Dad will make me say something about his watch, though," he reflected. And his hand went to his cheek where the bruise like a bunch of grapes still stretched. It had been as big as a bunch of bananas once, so it was shrinking.

"Has someone been ill-treating you?" Giles had asked him, and Joe, who ought to have welcomed the question (so eager was he usually for any attention), had resented it. He rubbed his bruise now, remembering Giles. "I don't want help from that gentleman."

He was a boy who had a good vocabulary and was quite sensitive in his use of words. He used the word 'gentleman' of Giles with a certain comfortable sense of irony. The word suited Giles, but yet at the same time, it reduced him to a bit of a joke.

"Gentleman," he repeated sleepily; he felt comfortable and relaxed. The radio sang gently in his ear, the sun shone on him on his grubby bed, and he drifted back to sleep.

The house was quiet and still. The rest of Hogie's Lane awoke to the day, got up, and set about their work. The Loudens were regarded as foreigners in Hogie's Lane. They had no close friends; but they were watched. Hogie's Lane knew that Rina Louden had a regular visitor once or twice a month. They also knew that Rina was away herself quite often. "Here today and gone tomorrow," was how they described Rina.

If they had been asked, say by Giles or Sergeant Santonelli, they would have said that in their opinion Rina was away now, and not sick at all.

Hogie's Lane was on the outskirts of the old town. Once it had been near the open fields and hills but now the new town (even Murreinhead had a new town) was ringing it in. The field which last year had grown cabbages now had forty bungalows disposed upon it. But the bungalows turned their backs on Hogie's Lane so that it was not overlooked. The main road from Murreinheadport passed the bungalows and then crossed the end of Hogie's Lane. Buses and lorries made this an increasingly busy road. At midday it was at its busiest.

A lorry, a battered dirty old lorry, not one of the newest sort, stopped at the side of the road, a man got out and the lorry went on. Nothing actually dropped out of the back of the lorry or fell from its frame or engine but it gave the impression this might happen at any moment.

"Old bone shaker," said the man who had got out. "Fall to bits one day. As long as it doesn't bite me when it does."

He walked down Hogie's Lane, not looking round him; it was his regular time to come, he was not much interested, he knew all there was to see.

He let himself into the house quietly with his key. But Joseph heard him and woke at once.

"Turn that bloody noise off."

"It is off, Dad."

"It is now."

"If you had wings, you'd fly away. I can see it on

87

your face," said his father sitting down on the end of the bed. "You're just like your mother. Where is Rina?" He looked round the room.

"Sh."

"I'm not shouting."

"No," said Joe miserably. Perhaps the voice was not loud: it was very penetrating, though.

"You look sick."

"Rina's been sick."

"Yes, well, you were expecting me," he stood up. "Although no one would know it from the welcome I got."

He walked round the room, which was untidy and dirty. He himself was neatly dressed.

"You can't live with Rina," he said, still walking round. "Even if I'd had a different job, one you came home from every night, I'd have had to move out. I couldn't have stood it. I wonder you stand it."

"I don't have much choice."

His father went over to a cupboard and pulled out a heavy case. "I've come to get my things, like I said," he threw the case on the bed and opened it. Everything in it was neat and tidy like all his possessions and none of Rina's. He started to check through his things methodically. His son eyed him.

"I'll be away about six weeks this time. A good run, though." His hands still in the case, he stared around him. "Where is Rina? Rina! Rina!"

"Dad…" Joe was shouting slightly himself. His voice was urgent. "Dad, I've lost your watch."

"What? What's that?"

"I borrowed your watch. And it got lost. I lost it."

"Liar. Liar," shouted his father. "I know the value of that watch. You and her sold it."

"No," Joe was almost weeping. "I lost it."

"And *that's* why Rina's gone off," said his father almost triumphantly. "She's not here. She's cleared off."

Joe was silent.

Sergeant Santonelli, standing quietly in the police station behind the crush desk by which the police of Murreinhead barricaded themselves against the populace of the town in case they should rush in and riot, looked up and saw a strange man at the door. He, too, like Giles and Joseph Louden, had memories of his day in court yesterday. His memories were different from both of theirs. He remembered it as the day when it felt as though a wolf had been eating at his entrails.

"I picked something up," he told himself, grateful that today he felt better.

Perhaps his indisposition marred his memories of the day, for he found that he couldn't remember it in detail, the way he usually could. Great cloudy gaps puzzled him. He had the impression he had said something outrageous to Giles Almond. Or perhaps told the truth about something he usually kept quiet. It was this he found most disquieting.

Every man has a secret face which he shows to no one, and now Santonelli had the sensation that he had not only shown this to Giles but that it had spoken.

"Probably shouted out loud," he reflected gloomily. "But what?" He could hardly go up to Giles and say: "What cat did I let out of what bag?"

He watched the man approach.

A visitor to the town, he thought.

"I've come to report the loss of a watch," said the man.

"What sort of a watch?" said Santonelli with a yawn.

"A gold Longines watch with a gold bracelet. Nine carat."

"That's a good watch." Santonelli stopped yawning. "Where did you lose it?"

"I don't know where exactly."

"That's a help," he pulled a pencil towards him. "What's your name and where do you live?"

"James Louden. I'm a seaman. I live aboard." "Aboard what?" Santonelli's pencil was poised.

"The *Black Princess*. She's a collier. We ply between here and London. But sometimes we go farther afield."

And that's how you got the watch, thought Santonelli.

"*Sure* you lost this watch in Murreinhead?"

"No. I'm not sure. My son had it, ye see."

Something in his voice made Santonelli ask the next question sharply.

"It was lost and not stolen?"

"I think it was stolen," said James Louden slowly. "I think my wife stole it."

"Your son had it and your wife stole it?" said the sergeant sceptically.

"That's the way it was."

And so in this way an essential piece of misinformation got into the police records.

Chapter 6

"WE DIDN'T get much from Murreinhead," said Coffin to his sergeant. "About the coat slashings. Nothing more come in while I was away.

Dove shook his head. "No more cases either. Not reported anyway. I don't believe there have been any. Word would have got round," he sounded uninterested.

"Still hot, isn't it?" said Coffin, pushing up a window.

"Hotter, if anything. It's better with that shut, you know. Only lets in the dust."

"It hasn't led to anything worse yet."

"What hasn't?" Dove had the window closed and latched. Like all the Dove family he preferred a good closed room.

"The coat slashing." "You still going on like that? I thought before it was just a forerunner of you being ill."

"I was sick," said Coffin irritably. "Sick in my stomach. Not wrong in my head."

Dove looked slightly shocked. Stomachs were not lightly spoken of in his hypochondriacal family.

"I didn't..." began Dove.

"You haven't learned to mask your feelings very well," said Coffin. But he was no longer irritated, only amused. "And now, for instance, you are thinking I ought to be preparing a report for the conference tomorrow and at the same time planning how to eat humble pie because we've had a bank robber loose in the manor for ten days and haven't caught him yet."

"I was thinking it was time we had another patrol down Herring Creek Alley," said Dove. "You know we used to put on a search down there automatically in the old days when we'd lost someone. The bank boy could be hiding out down there. It's the ideal place, real rabbit warren and access to the river and the railway line."

"He's a high-class boy, this one, he wouldn't be hanging out in Herring Creek Alley."

"You can't tell," persisted Dove.

"And the reason we've left Herring Creek Alley alone lately," Coffin reminded him, "is that the place hasn't been the same since they knocked down the feather warehouse and put up a big block of council flats."

"It still smells the same down there to my way of thinking," said Dove, whose blood and inheritance made him nothing if not obstinate. "And as for the block of flats, one of the Cuttance boys moved in there six months ago."

There was silence for a moment. The Cuttances were one of the criminal clans of Coffin's district. The other was the Flemings. But the Cuttances were the biggest and the best.

"What made *him* eligible for a council flat?" said Coffin irritably.

"He's got triplet sons. *They* made him eligible."

"Someone ought to have blackballed him."

"Be reasonable. It's not a club."

"It will be by now. Cuttance's club."

"That's what I was saying."

"It should never have been allowed."

"Oh, the probation officer spoke up for Binky, said what a good boy he was now, and how good he was going to be. He's only eighteen you know."

"Still? He seems to have been eighteen for years. How old's his wife?"

"Twenty-three."

"Oh, the happy happy summers we've got in front of us with Binky and his triplet sons," said Coffin "Well, let's run our hands over Herring Creek Alley and see what we pull out and I'll go and eat my humble pie before the Wenlayden."

Coffin's sub-division had recently acquired a new boss, Bill Wenlayden. His manners, tastes and temper were so far only known by reputation, but the outlook was not promising. Ahead of every senior policeman goes a penumbra made up of gossip, legend and jokes. Every man has his signature and his subordinates know how to recognise it. What Coffin did not know was that, as men trained by him moved around, he himself was rapidly building up a myth of his own. People told the story of how he had followed a wanted man all over the Battersea Fun Fair, or down river to the Blackheath August Bank Holiday Fair, and arrested him for bigamy in the Tunnel of Love. How he walked into a burning house to get out the man he wanted, who had later hung. How he had married... but the stories were not true, or only partly true, and did not relate to the real Coffin.

Coffin went for a walk through his district that evening, through the crowded centre streets, crossing the great main road that cut it into two, and moving closer to the river. He was hatless and carrying his jacket. The heat was greater than ever as midsummer approached.

The street market around the Red Bull was still going strong, late as it was. This side of the road was crowded, but the other side of the road, where Coffin was walking, was empty. He felt as though he was the only man alive on this side of the road. At the same time, he had the strange sensation that he was watching a stage set, that what he was seeing was a play put on. But not necessarily put on for his amusement. No. In fact, when he thought about it, he had the feeling that a bigger and more impersonal audience was looking on, that the whole production was on a much larger scale than he guessed, and that he was only a fly that had crawled on the stage.

So he walked alone, watching with detached eyes the stream of people passing in both directions, all different and yet; all the same. A fat woman pushed past another fat woman so like her as to be almost her twin and yet apparently without seeing the resemblance. Two young women guiding prams and swinging white handbags wove politely around each other, nodding politely as if they were partners in a dance but remaining aloof. Two girls with swinging hair approached each other and then walked on but without acknowledging the mirror image. There's only one of me, thought Coffin, secure on his side of the street. Then he looked round him hastily to make sure.

"And that's the house where they had the poltergeist," he pointed out to himself, creating an echo where none was. "And that's the stall where the owner was making his own florin pieces in his cellar... I see he's out of prison again and still doing nicely. Wonder what he's up to this time?" He paused for a moment to watch. Even across the width of the road the strength of his gaze seemed to make itself felt and the stall-owner looked across and saw him. Apparently what he saw gave him small pleasure, for he at once turned his back and started to pack up his stall.

But perhaps Coffin was only imagining this. For when he looked back the stall was busy as ever and the owner was holding up a length of silk to an elderly woman. Coffin gave his head a shake to clear it.

Coffin walked on. It was shady and quiet on this side. Across the street an ice-cream man was selling cornets and lemonade. Next to him was a flower stall with roses. Coffin stood and looked at the roses. They bloomed in the evening light, golden and indestructible. As he looked, he saw that they *were* indestructible. Every flower on the stall was plastic.

"Couldn't expect the Red to have *real* roses," he told himself sadly.

"This is just the sort of night the Slasher might

be out. Might even get ambitious. Branch out, indulge his fancy."

For there was a hint of a sinister fancy there, he felt sure.

"Supposing things got out of control. My control? Or his?" Beneath the sultry heat there was a threat of thunder.

The crowd across the road was thinner down this end, and one or two people were beginning to stand out: the tall man with the enormous mane of fuzzy hair standing smoking at the corner of Pickle Herring Street; the pretty girl giggling at her plain friend; the woman walking steadily through the crowd, carrying a huge carton of empty beer bottles.

There *was* someone on his side of the street.

Coffin looked around quickly, feeling rather than seeing the movement behind him.

It was a lame old dog, limping gently along, quietly self-absorbed.

Coffin felt put in his place by the old animal's indifference. Whatever he was in the dog's world— a smell, a moving shape—he was nothing important.

His attention was suddenly caught by a woman moving across the scene. She was alone and walking slowly. She did not move in a straight line but let her progress take her almost aimlessly from side to side of the pavement. At one moment she was staring in a shop window and then at the next she was at the kerb studying a stall. Her very aimlessness made her stand out in the crowd because most of those surrounding her were pressing on with at least the air of having somewhere to go.

"What's she up to?" He could at once think of several causes for her behaviour, but none of them seemed to fit. Now she was almost opposite him he could see she was a tall, pretty, young woman. She continued to walk alone, peering at things in a shortsighted way and with a small half smile on her lips.

For a second Coffin asked himself if they had a decoy out tonight and she was it. But he dismissed the question even as it formed in his mind. She was not a policewoman, whoever she was.

Without knowing it, he was keeping pace with her now as she walked, so that they were almost level.

But the word decoy began to drag up from a lower level the worry that was forming there inarticulately.

She's asking for trouble, thought Coffin. If the Slasher is around, then she's just the sort he'd go for. Now that he looked at her again, he thought that she had a secret sickly face, the sort of face that might stimulate some men to violence.

"She looks, oh, she looks as if she would hang around and wait for you to beat her." To his discomfort he found he was becoming angry with her. He wrenched his head round so that he need not see her. The dog had hurried on and was now trotting in front of him.

He turned his eyes back; she was still weaving her way through the crowd but there were fewer and fewer people and she stood out even more clearly as an individual. He noticed that her head was very slightly inclined to one side, in a pose that accentuated the slight curve of her lips, too ambiguous really to be called a smile. She was wearing a cotton dress with very prominent red and white stripes.

Some yards down the street, in the more crowded part, he saw a man hurrying. He seemed to have his eyes fixed on the figure in the red and white dress.

"I believe he's following her."

He watched; the distance between the two walkers never altered.

He himself crossed over the road so that he was on the same side of the road. He placed himself so that he was third in the procession. A few hundred yards ahead the character of the road changed abruptly. The stalls stopped, the lights seemed fewer, and a great high brick wall dominated the street. A side road cut sharply cut towards the canal.

Coffin swore softly to himself. Killeghan's Walk. In that district they called this dark slit of a street Kill-the-Girl-Walk. Of course, she was making for that street. A girl with a face and a fortune like that must be making for Killeghan's Walk.

He hurried his pace.

The girl paused, at the point where the dark street

began. She half turned. She seemed to point with her hand.

The pointing finger, the smile, the half turn of the body, all added up to something sinister.

"She is *willing* herself to be attacked," he had a sudden picture of her body sagging to the pavement, skirts twisted and bloody.

He began to run.

Seeing him run (and he was, after all, known by many to be a policeman), the people around him began to stare.

The girl had reached the corner of Killeghan's Walk and her follower was very close behind when they both stopped.

"I thought you was never going to catch me up," said the girl in a hoarse voice. "I've been beckoning and beckoning you to hurry up but there you go, dreaming along as usual. Mum'll be ever so cross if we're late for supper."

They both turned and stared as Coffin came up, mouths open, gaping in surprise.

I was obsessed with my own ideas. Mad, thought Coffin, as he walked on past them, ignoring them. He was shaken that he could have got a situation so wrong. Almost as if I'm sick. Perhaps it's a hangover from being ill.

There was no harm in the situation at all. He could see now that they were sister and young brother on their way home. How could he have failed to see that the man wasn't a man at all but only a young boy? The girl might not be a very nice girl (even now he thought there was something neurotic and wrong about her expression) but for the moment anyway she was behaving normally.

He turned back and started to walk home.

A little later he stopped to look in the window of the little sweetshop opposite Creevey Buildings. There was something soothing and tranquil about the boxes of chocolates and jars of sweets. Patsy would like some chocolates. Ignoring his knowledge that Patsy was on a strict diet, he went into the shop. There was a small plump woman in there already, talking to the shopkeeper. She was sitting comfortably on a chair with her handbag on her lap and she looked as if she had been there some time, more like a visitor than a customer. When Coffin came in, she made a token gesture of getting up and acting as if to go.

"Oh, don't you go, Maisie," said the proprietor. "You haven't finished telling me." She looked at Coffin expectantly. "Yes?"

"A box of chocolate ginger. Plain chocolate," he said anxiously. His Patsy's palate could only take the darkest bitterest chocolate.

"Well, I dunno if I've got those." She turned away to look, giving the search only half her attention, though. "Know what they're going to put up over there, Maisie?" she said, nodding with her head towards the window and across the road.

"Over where?" Maisie had her handbag open and was looking for something. "I've got this letter to show you. It just explains everything about that..."

"Creevey Buildings." She had found a box of chocolate ginger. "They're going to stick up a skyscraper with a car park on the top. On the top, mind you, Maisie. They call it a 'project'."

"I don't see how they'll get the cars up there," said Maisie deliberately. She laid aside her search for the letter.

"Oh, they'll use lifts. The chocolates are twelve shillings, sir."

"Well, I didn't think they'd walk," said Maisie. "That *would* be a project."

"I don't think these chocolates look fresh."

"Try another box then. Yes. they do look a little bit scratched, don't they?" She examined the box.

"Oh, I dare say the rats have been at them then," said Maisie. "Ever since Creevey Buildings have been empty, we've had nothing but rats, rats, rats, over our side of the road. I'll be glad when the whole building's gone and everything's cleared out, rats, and all."

"I haven't noticed any rats."

"Oh, you don't notice anything."

"Well, I won't take these chocolates anyway," said Coffin. He added, "Thank you."

"I'll get you another box, sir, you don't have to take it seriously, what she said about rats. She didn't mean it."

"Yes, I did," said Maisie stoutly.

"I'll just take a packet of mints." It didn't look as though the rats had got their teeth into them. He paid for them and left, hearing the shop woman say to Maisie as he turned away: "Go on about Mrs Biggins's daughter, Maisie."

The sunlight was still shining on the upper floors of Creevey Buildings, making the window panes glitter.

"I've always liked the old building myself," Coffin said, half aloud. "It's been a part of my life."

He walked inside. The great hallway and high stone staircase were echoing and empty. He coughed and a hollow sound came back to him.

At the bottom of the stairs he looked up. It must be about ten years since he had stood here last and looked up this stone flight and seen a murderer coming down, and it was a good deal longer since he had played as a boy around these bleak halls. One of his best friends had lived on the second floor. The friend was dead now and anyway had ceased to acknowledge John Coffin as a friend long before his death. Perhaps it was a mistake to be a policeman in the district where you had grown up.

Once, just after his friend Peter died, John Coffin had visited his mother. As far as he knew she was still alive and had probably gone on living here on her own until rehoused a few weeks ago. He remembered her as a plump, red-faced, cheerful woman who had given him chocolate cake and tea just as if he was still a boy of thirteen and not even then an anxious policeman. "I'm sorry about Peter," he had said.

"Well, he asked for it. If you go around with the sort of people he did, then you ask to be knifed one day. And he was."

Knifed was the word she used. Probably it was the stirring of the memory in his mind that had brought him here on this day.

He walked slowly up the stairs. The second floor looked much the same as it always had done. There were still the chips in the marbled walls which they had kicked with their football boots. He stood there uncertainly, the thirteen-year-old boy, the young police sergeant and the mature John Coffin all jostling inside him. A memory came back to him that had been buried for years.

On this flight of stairs he had seen two old people, a man and a woman, having a fight. It had been his first introduction to the cruelty and roughness of his district.

Times have changed, he thought. You wouldn't see it now. I hope.

On the next landing the old dog was lying, eyes alert, ears pricked. At no time could he have been a beautiful animal, he had never resembled any known breed, and at this moment he looked like an embittered old hearthrug. He didn't quite growl when he saw Coffin but he showed his teeth. "Hello, old boy," said Coffin, patting his head. Quite a brave thing to do in the circumstances. He looked around. "Do you live here? Or did you live here once? Did your family move out and leave you behind?"

He rubbed his hand over the dog's rough coat. "What an odd mixture you are. I don't believe you're a dog at all, really, just something furry on legs. And with teeth," he added, hastily withdrawing his fingers.

The dog got up and moved a few feet, then turned and looked back at him.

"Don't tell me you're leading me to your aged sick master, or your little lost mistress," said Coffin ironically. "You don't look a story-book dog to me."

But he followed as the dog led him forward. Together they went to the end of the corridor and up the next flight of stairs, the old animal looking behind at intervals to see if Coffin was following.

"I believe you are leading me somewhere."

They got to the top of the stairs. The dog watched Coffin reach the top of the flight, and then blandly trotted over to the pile of sacks, where he lay down and turned bright eyes on his follower.

"I might have known you were a dead-end dog," said Coffin. "I could easily get fed up with you."

The dog closed his eyes and appeared to go to sleep. Slowly, and now alone, Coffin continued his tour of exploration. Nothing was easy to see in the twilight but he had an impression of staircases that wound on and on forever and dark marbled corridors running off them endlessly.

"This was a clean building once," he said. "Now it smells of old rubbish."

Nearly all the doors stood open, including the door to the flat where his friends had lived. He looked at it but did not go in. Which was now real? The living room where he had eaten chocolate cake and felt the warmth of a coal fire? Or the now desolate empty place he would see if he looked? Instead, impelled like Bluebeard's wife to the one door that was closed, he went to the first door on the top floor and opened it.

He knew at once that someone had been camping out in these rooms since they had been evacuated by their original rent-paying inhabitants. This last lot had not paid rent and had not been very careful in their habits.

In fact the room smelt.

There was a pseudo-inhabitant there now.

On the couch an old coat and hat had been draped. Coffin was drawn towards them because he thought in a macabre way that they were arranged in the shape of a body.

The smell was much worse as he drew nearer.

Chapter 7

GILES, lying in his narrow bed, groaned. The groans woke him up. He tried to move his body and it felt strangely empty, as if it could not respond to him.

He coughed and something strange happened. A little warm wet patch appeared under his fingers, which lay on his chest.

"That felt like a bubble," said Giles. It was a ridiculous thing to say and he knew it. So he made it more sensible by adding: "A bubble of blood."

Then a degree more of consciousness came back and he knew he was not lying on his bed but on the hard floor of his cold hall, and that the groan which was now coming up through his throat was a real groan, and he was in pain.

He gave another loud groan and propped himself up against the wall. He looked at the blood on his hand.

"Not dead yet, anyway," he said aloud. He made it sound oddly jaunty, and, indeed, deep below his shock and pain, something hopeful was rising.

Sitting up, he felt at once physically weaker and much clearer in the head.

He knew precisely what had happened to him. He had been working late the night before. He experienced a moment's confusion before he succeeded in placing himself accurately in time. Since the meeting of the Burgh Court on Tuesday, he had been working hard every night; it was now either Friday night or Saturday morning. He looked round, conscious of his feebleness: it was Saturday morning.

The restlessness of the last few days had expressed itself not only in hard work but in long walks round the town. He hardly knew why he was so restless. Sometimes he blamed it on the heat, sometimes on a sort of irritability with himself and his achievements that came on him. And beneath this irritability was a sense of failure. He wanted to be a success, to stand well in the world, and yet he drew back from the struggle that was necessary. He did not want to compete. Perhaps he was frightened to compete. But underneath all this was a specific worry. He was worried about the case of Robertina Louden and Lizzie Hamilton. He had heard that Lizzie Hamilton had tried twice to call on Rina Louden. Apparently Mrs Louden's door had remained shut. But he had also heard that the boy had been seen walking through the town with fresh bruises... There was some trouble about a watch, according to Santonelli.

"Funny situation in that family," Santonelli had commented. "Father don't trust mother, son don't trust father, mother—well, she's a big question mark but the only time I saw her I got the impression she didn't trust anyone. And who's to say any one of them are wrong?" He had no hopes of finding the missing watch: he did not think Louden expected him to find the watch. No, behind the problem of the watch was something else again.

So, almost without thinking, Giles's long walks had taken him down Hogie's Lane and past the house where the Loudens lived. More and more Giles found himself thinking: "where they are *alleged* to live." But the boy was there. Once he saw his face at the window.

On Friday night Giles came home and went into his dark house. He pushed the front door shut behind him without looking.

But it would not shut. And at the feeling of the counter-pressure, he turned his head slowly.

"Too slowly," said Giles aloud and with some bitterness. But once again, irrepressibly, the small note sounded inside him. He had fought back bravely.

"I think I must have marked him."

Even as he said it a question began to form in his mind.

Him? Who was this him of whom his memory spoke?

Giles closed his eyes and tried to see the figure. Santonelli was going to want a description. But all that came to him was an impression of a curiously bulky shape. Oddly enough, his strongest memory was of the *feel*, the strange softness of his attacker. Santonelli was going to ask questions about that too.

His head felt very heavy.

When he opened his eyes again, Santonelli was staring down at him.

"You're a fine one," said Santonelli. "Good job

Eleanor found you lying there."

"Eh? Eleanor?"

"She's the girl who delivers your papers. She looked through your letterbox and saw you."

"Good old Eleanor," muttered Giles. "I don't know Eleanor."

"She admires you." Santonelli was on his knees, competently examining the wound. "Not so bad as I thought," he said, his voice relieved. "I think he must have hit you on the head as well and that's why you lay like the dead," he ran his hand over Giles's head. Giles winced. "Or else you knocked yourself when you fell. Yes, that's it."

"But I behaved bravely."

"Is that important?" said Santonelli irritably. He had been worried, and relief made him edgy.

"To me it is," said Giles, choking.

Santonelli gave him some water. "Doctor's coming," he said.

"Because for me it helps cancel out what happened in London."

"The doctor's coming," repeated Santonelli; he had started to look worried again. He himself would only have started to talk as Giles was now if he was dying.

"It makes something better that was bad."

"I don't know what you mean."

"I'll tell you later," said Giles, still gasping. "Some time, perhaps."

Very soon after his arrival, the doctor had examined Giles and he reported that the stab wound was from a knife.

Santonelli looked impatient. "It's not bad enough," went on the doctor. "Just a slit across the belly," he sounded almost cheerful. "Didn't go in. I've sewn you up and you'll do fine. Sore and stiff, though. No walking about, mind."

"I shouldn't dream of it," said Giles. He was comfortably tucked up in bed in his great bed in his elegant but bare bedroom. "I might starve but I won't walk about."

"Ach, you won't starve," said Santonelli. He was looking out of the window. "The women will be all over you. They'll be in and out with dishes of food. You'll be a godsend to them. I had the flu once and I lived like a lord. I tell you I was better looked after than a king. Better than I am now I'm married," he added: "My Jean was the first. I was married to her within the year…"

"I don't advise too much eating," said the doctor, preparing to go. "Remember that. Not too much eating," he closed his bag. "I'll look in on you tomorrow.

"I'm thinking what to do," said Santonelli, as he looked down on his friend. "You're all right now."

"I hope."

"You are."

He closed the door quietly behind him, then came back for a last word.

"Just mark who it is brings you the first tray of

111

food. Just mark, that's all."

In London the doctors and the police also had a problem, but the heat had made it impossible for them to be as succinct as the doctor in Murreinhead. Decomposition was far advanced in the body discovered by John Coffin in Creevey Buildings. There was no sign, however, of the rats having been at work, so perhaps they had moved out.

The demolition of Creevey Buildings was indefinitely suspended while the police swarmed all over it.

"It's an act of God," said the old man who sold newspapers across the road. "They'll never shift the old Creevey now," he sounded triumphant as if he had placed himself on the side of all those dark forces which seem sometimes to appear from nowhere to direct our lives. His God, you could tell from the sound of his voice, was faceless and nameless.

"That's a sneaky way to talk," reproved his customer. "I don't like it."

"Ah, *she* knows, she knows, the one they've found up there," said the old man. He knew, before anyone else, that the dead person was a woman.

In a short while, the police doctor confirmed this fact: the body was that of an unidentified woman, aged probably between thirty-five and forty. She had been dead about two weeks.

"Some time on the weekend of May 29th." Coffin was told. "Give or take a day or two."

"I understand."

"And she was stabbed. She was stabbed three times, once in the throat, once in the chest and once in the abdomen. Any one of these wounds could have killed her."

"Would she have survived if anyone could have got to her in time?"

There was a pause. They were talking over the telephone, and Coffin was watching Sergeant Dove's face, which was drained of all feeling and expression except pain as he touched his heel, on which heat and sweat had brought up a huge blister.

"No, probably not," said the voice at the end of the telephone. "No, I don't see how she could have done. She was stabbed in the room where you found her; she collapsed and died pretty quickly. No one moved her after death. No, you've nothing to reproach yourself with."

"Except that I knew something bad was coming and didn't know how to stop it," said Coffin half aloud, half under his breath. He was visited again by another of his vivid mental pictures: this time of the woman sinking to the ground with blood pouring from her and her killer running out of the room and down the stone stairs.

"Eh?" said Dove; he had stopped prodding the blister and was unobtrusively slipping his shoe back on.

"Weekend of the twenty-ninth," said Coffin, eyeing the calendar. "The weekend of the bag snatchings. It's connected, you know. Must be."

"I don't see the *must*."

"And if so, with Murreinhead possibly. Why haven't we heard from Murreinhead?" said Coffin irritably.

He looked balefully at the telephone, which did not ring. Nor did it ring on the next day, which was Sunday, June 14th. Santonelli was still wondering what he ought to do. On Monday he telephoned London.

"I'm not saying, mind you," he said, "that there's any proven connection between our coat slashing up here and your bag snatching down there. Doesn't seem likely really, but since you're interested, I'm informing you that a man up here has been stabbed."

"Where?" asked Coffin. "Where was he stabbed?"

"In the belly," said the slow Scots voice with just a hint of yet another accent which Coffin could not then quite place. "But he fought the attacker off and he'll do nicely. It was a nasty thing though, you understand."

"I'm glad he's not dead," began Coffin.

"Och no, not dead at all. But he doesn't know who knifed him."

"No." He was just about to go on to say that neither did the woman who had been stabbed to death in London when he reflected that this might not be true. She might very well have known and perhaps know well the person who had stabbed her. She must have gone to meet her killer in that room where she had died. Or perhaps she was just followed. Then he heard Santonelli say:

"But we have the knife."

"They have the knife," he repeated to Dove, in surprise. It had somehow never seemed likely that the knife would ever turn up. "They have found the knife."

"They have found *a* knife," said Dove, who did not believe in going further than his facts allowed.

Giles was up early on Monday morning and moving stiffly around. The stiffness was physical and not emotional. He felt very happy.

He had slept most of Saturday and only awoke in the evening to see his door slowly opening. Catriona stood there. She was quite alone, but no doubt she felt adequately chaperoned by the huge supper tray she was carrying.

"I've brought you a little food," she said calmly, whipping off the white cloth that covered the tray, and revealing soup, fish, a covered dish with steam escaping, a pot of cream, fruit and a little decanter.

I always knew Willie kept a good table, was Giles's instantaneous thought. There was food here for several men. He found his mouth watering.

"Aye, you'll be wanting it," went on Catriona. "Father and I both thought so."

115

She did not collect the tray herself, instead the little servant-girl came, but Catriona reappeared with food twice the next day, always self-possessed, always unemotional.

Contrary to what the sergeant had predicted, there was absolutely no sign of any other visitors.

"I don't know what I'd do without you," said Giles, as this thought crossed his mind.

"Oh, there were plenty of others wanting." said Catriona cheerfully, "but I frightened them off."

Giles lay in bed and considered this all through the long Sunday evening, while the town church played its carillon to celebrate a long-ago victory of its local regiment on a distant Indian frontier. Murreinhead never made any bones about its pugnacity. The note of triumph which he had felt earlier became stronger and steadier.

Meanwhile the woman in London remained unidentified. Already the police had noticed that she had no handbag.

Shrewd guesses would soon be made about her identity; the remains of her handbag would eventually be resurrected, but a much more intractable problem remained. How and why had she come to Creevey Buildings? What was she doing in this place at all?

Chapter 8

HOW DID SHE come to be lying dead in this room in Creevey Buildings, South London? As soon as you thought about it, the problem assumed a more monstrous shape.

Creevey Buildings had been gradually emptied of its tenants over the last six months. For the last six weeks it was supposed by the local housing authority who owned it to be entirely empty. But as the old dwellers moved out, others drifted in. It was always easy to get into Creevey Buildings, the flimsy padlocks and old chains offered hardly any resistance to the determined and in any case they could always be ignored and you could shin up a drainpipe and go in through an upper storey window. The second wave of inhabitants were not too proud to enter through a broken window. As the police went systematically over the building, they found clear traces of the invaders. In one room were the remains of a fire with a pot of food still on it; in another room the old mattress which was the bed was still warm. They actually found one of the new inhabitants hiding in a cupboard. He was a small timid West Indian wearing a white cotton hat. He said he had moved into Creevey Buildings because it was cheap.

"Free, you mean," said Dove. "But not at the price you'll pay."

The two men, one dark-skinned, and one pink and hot, looked at each other.

"You think just because you're coloured I'll let you

nip off and no harm done," said Dove, gifted with sudden prescience.

"We are all coloured," said his captive politely. "I am one colour, you are another. You are pink. Very, very pink."

Dove growled.

"And of course I will not ask you to let me go free. You will not do it and I will not ask."

"You can go, though," said Dove, unexpectedly mildly. "You can clear off for the time being. I'll show you where to get a room for the night and I'll know where to find you."

"Oh, I know *that* place. They don't make any charge, but they don't let me out in the morning either."

"No. Not prison," said Dove in a patient voice. "Hospital. You're sick, aren't you?"

There was at once a stiffness and yet a languor in the man's movements: he was excessively thin but his face was puffy. This was something a person like Dove could not miss.

"What are your symptoms? Thirsty, eh? Drink a lot?"

The man shrugged. But his tongue licked his lips nervously.

Outside in the corridors of Creevey Buildings even the noises attendant upon a full-scale murder investigation gave ground before the intimation of a mortal illness. There was no way out of this case except through the hospital or the morgue. Dove felt ill himself.

118

"Why was she here? Why did she die here? What do you think, Dove?"

Coffin was walking up and down the narrow ill-lit room. He picked up an empty tin that had contained pineapple in syrup. It was old and full of flies; some of the flies were shrivelled and dead.

"Someone was living in this room. But was it her?" But when you said someone was living in this room, the word living had to be handled with care. It meant living like a cave dweller.

"No, her clothes are all wrong. She was wearing clean, new clothes when she died. She wasn't living here, yet she came here. Why?"

"I'm not so sure she wasn't living here." Dove was turning over the objects in a cardboard box. He had a lipstick in his hands. Also in the box were a tom handkerchief, a packet of cigarettes, an old piece of towel and an empty aspirin bottle. There was also a cup without a handle, a grubby silk scarf and a powder-puff At least two of these objects, the scarf and the powderpuff, were indisputably feminine. "I mean, some of these things look as though she had a foothold here."

"No one admits to seeing her come here. And yet you'd think there was a chance someone would have seen her."

Dove shrugged. He knew well enough, and thought Coffin should know by now, the constitutional blindness of the district. Perhaps

119

someone had seen her but preferred to keep quiet. "We don't have much of a description to offer."

"We have something." Coffin consulted a typewritten paper. "She was a well-built woman, height five foot five inches, weight about 130 pounds, dark curly hair and blue eyes. She was wearing a red cotton dress with a stiff underskirt and white shoes. The dress was printed with little red birds on a white ground. No hat. No bag."

He considered. "No bag. Something to think about there."

"The West Indian I picked up didn't see anything," observed Dove. "He wouldn't, of course. But he said that he'd noticed a new smell up there from the night of Saturday, May 30th. He notices smells, you see, being sick."

"He notices dates, too," said Coffin suspiciously.

"Yes. I pressed him on that; he said he has to know the date or he feels lost. It's all he's got, you see—this day he's alive."

"You and your invalids," grumbled Coffin. "We can't do much about a smell. There was a smell when I got there too. A different one, I expect."

"You don't have to set any store by it." Dove was equable. "Anyway, he said it smelt like a fire."

"Oh, that is a help," said Coffin bitterly. "A fire. There's absolutely no sign of a fire. What sort of fire? Coal or wood?"

"Probably just someone having a smoke," agreed Dove. "But we can ask him again."

"Where is he?" "In the Men's Free." The South

London Men's Free Hospital was an institution well known to Dove, many of whose relations, persecuted by poor health as they were, had been visited by him there. "They took him in at once. They were glad to get him." Dove often spoke of the doctors and hospitals as grateful, even eager, to get their hands on patients. Perhaps he really did think he was doing a doctor a favour when he called for his services. "He's a case and a half, he is. They won't get another like him in a hurry."

"Was she sick, do you think?" asked Coffin, going back suddenly to his big problem. "Could she have been sick?"

What is it makes me think that? His eyes fell on the aspirin bottle. He picked it up. On the bottom was a small white chemist's label. The label was torn but one word clearly stood out. Murreinhead.

The case of Agnes Dyke against Alexander Knowles: adjourned.

The case of the Police against Peter Robert Bell: adjourned.

The case of Lizzie Hamilton and Robertina Louden: a question mark.

A knife lay on the table in front of Sergeant Santonelli in Murreinhead police station. This knife would shortly be going to Glasgow for forensic examination. After this it might take a further trip to London. It depended. The forensic report and photographs certainly would go. He, for his part, had a set of photographs, which had come to him from London with a query from John Coffin. These were photographs of the dead woman. This knife had certainly cut Giles Almond; had it any connection with the slashing of Robertina Louden's coat? He had to ask himself that question but he could not give it the force of reality. Rina Louden and her son, and possibly her husband too, were rootless, feckless people by Santonelli's standards and he was uneasy at the thought of them.

"I canna get a grip on them," he muttered to himself. Nevertheless, he had taken several practical steps. He had sent a detective constable to check up on James Louden and his ship the *Black Princess*. He had sent a description of the missing watch to all the jewellers and pawnbrokers in the town and in Murreinheadport and in Glasgow. The watch had not turned up. Santonelli would have been very surprised if it had.

In Murreinhead, a knife.

In London, an aspirin bottle. And a dead woman.

Between the two there was a connection. Santonelli put on his hat and went round to the house where Rina Louden and her son lived. On the way there he saw Catriona Tulloch entering Giles Almond's house. She was wearing a flowered hat and looked as though she had just come from a garden party, but she was carrying a tray. He smiled. He prided himself on perception in these matters, and he had backed Catriona.

"Good girl," he said aloud.

Not being a romantic like Giles, Santonelli was not attracted by the Louden home and its neighbours. But he knew more than Giles about the shifting population of Hogie's Lane, and had a better appreciation of the problem it was for the police. Murreinhead was, with some notable reservations like Jamie the town drunk, a very quiet town; Murreinheadport was not. Hogie's Lane, on the main road between Murreinhead and Murreinheadport, and on the way to London, usually housed a few rejects or refugees from the bigger town. He thought Rina and her son had probably come from there. And were on their way where?

"Your mother?" he said to the boy Joseph, who opened the door.

"She's not in."

"No." Santonelli accepted this. He was already looking round the room in which he found himself.

"I didn't say you could come in."

"No." Santonelli accepted this too, shoving the boy a little aside. There was a casual violence in his manner that would have surprised Giles. The boy received it in a matter-of-fact way, and this at once gave him away to Santonelli as someone with his own little experience of the police to draw upon.

Poor little dwarf, he thought, but without pity. He's a man, but he hasn't got the weight. It did not make him more tender to the boy, rather the reverse, as if the boy was now somehow outside warranty, a kind of outlaw.

"Where is your mother?"

"Rina's away."

"Where? Away where?"

"I don't know."

"Oh, you know. You know something. She said something before she went."

The room was tidy but with a boy's tidiness. Teapot, jug, kettle, jam-jars and plates, all clean and neat in orderly rows, but nothing put away in a cupboard. Clothes arranged over every chair and a towel drying in the window, but the bed was made. He seemed to be living and sleeping in one room. Underneath it all was a long-standing disorder which he had probably been unable to do anything about.

"I didn't even see her go."

"Now come on, Joey, don't tell me that. If you didn't see her go you know where she is."

"My name is *Joseph.*' '

"That's a nice name," said Santonelli, not altogether pleasantly .

"It's my name." He said it aggressively.

"I'm not going to rob you of it. Your mother now, she's not here some of the time by the look of it. Why aren't you at school?"

"I'm over the age. I've been working."

"*Could* have been working, you mean."

"I've had jobs," said Joseph sullenly.

"Really quite suits you being here on your own."

Santonelli sat down as if he was prepared to wait a long time, perhaps till Rina Louden came back. He nodded his head towards the radio. "Turn that thing off, will you."

"It's not loud." This was true; it was not loud.

"It's persistent, though," he put out his hand and silenced it. "Practically red hot. Don't you ever turn it off? "

"Rina told me when she went off that she wouldn't be coming back," said the boy. He spoke suddenly and loudly, as if he had now resolved to talk.

"Did she now?"

"She was sick, Rina was. I mean she wasn't herself."

"And she took the watch with her?"

"The watch?" he stared. "Dad's watch? No, she didn't take the watch."

"Why did she say she wasn't coming back? Why do you think she said that?"

There was a pause while the boy considered. "She was frightened, I reckon," he said finally.

"About the business with Mrs Hamilton? About the case she was bringing?"

"She should never have said that," declared the boy. "Never."

"So it wasn't true?"

Joseph Louden did not answer.

Santonelli tried something else. "Have you got a photograph of your mother?"

"No. No."

"Well, don't act so fierce," said Santonelli, for once gentle. "I was trying to spare you something... As it is, you'll have to come with me. Oh no, no," as the boy started to move away, just to look at a picture.

"No. No pictures," he had started to cry. "Why should I? I won't."

"Look—your mother's missing, isn't she?"

"I didn't say so."

Santonelli waved his hand round the room. "Everything says so."

They both heard the front door open at the same time.

Just my luck if Rina Louden walks in this minute, thought Santonelli. He dearly wanted to be proved right, to be the one who got the correct answer. He *needed* to score. Never mind if to be right meant a rough episode for someone else.

"Joe!" called a voice. "Rina! Is that you? I came in on the usual wagon."

"He's calling you," said Santonelli.

"It's my dad."

"I know that."

He went out into the hall. James Louden was kneeling on the floor opening a cupboard.

"Here, what's up?" he said, still kneeling there. "If it's about that watch, forget it."

"It's too late to say that, Mr Louden."

"It's not about the watch, then," he sat back on his heels and looked sombre. "Well, go on then, shake it out, whatever you've got in your hand,

and let me have a look."

Santonelli hesitated.

"Come on, hurry up. Don't keep me waiting."

"No need to get angry, Mr Louden, I'm only doing my job."

"Big life," said James Louden.

"Do you want to find your wife or not, Mr Louden?" Santonelli ignored the sneer.

"My wife?" Louden sounded surprised. "She's not wanting, is she?"

"I don't know," said Santonelli. "She doesn't seem to be around."

Louden started his work on the cupboard again without answering. He was taking out what seemed to be somebody's wardrobe of old clothes.

Perhaps he's got her in there, thought Santonelli, madly.

"I'm collecting my togs to take away," said Louden, suddenly standing up. He dusted his hands on his trousers. "All right, I'll come with you."

Not once had he looked at his son.

In her front window Lal Jennings sat looking out. She was alone. The health visitor came, and her home help. But there was no Winnie.

Oddly enough, Lal had told no one about Winnie's defection. Or perhaps it wasn't odd. Lal was a stiff, reserved old woman, much turned in on herself by illness. And there had been the beginnings of a quarrel between the friends over Winnie's lodger. Once before Winnie had failed in her visits for a whole month and this bitter silent struggle between them had been, as also perhaps this time, due to Lal's acerbity. Victory was bound to come to Lal because she *could* not give way. She could only sit and wait.

And yet they were the closest of friends. Probably Winnie had no one else in the world she knew as she knew Lal. Certainly no one but Lal waited or watched for her.

Lal took both a morning and an evening paper and listened to every news bulletin to be heard on her radio. With her morning tea she read about the discovery of the woman's body in Creevey Buildings. She read it with interest while her home help, provided and paid for by the Health Service, but much harried by Lal, cleaned the room and made the bed.

The evening paper was brought in by the nurse, who put her to bed and made her a drink of cocoa. (There had been a time when Lal had stood out for ale or anyway stout, which was so good for you; but that battle was over and it was one that Lal had lost.) Lal read the paper silently. There was no description of the woman's face, because for various reasons this would have been difficult, but there was a description of her clothes. She had been wearing a red and white cotton dress with a stiff underskirt. It sounded an ordinary enough description but to this reader it meant something.

"That's Winnie's lodger," said Lal, putting down the paper.

"Eh?" said her nurse. "Don't spill the cocoa, there's a good girl." She always called Lal her 'good girl' which made Lal want to bite her. She *had* bitten her once, and pretended it was an accident.

"It's Winnie's lodger," repeated Lal, rapping the paper. "I'd know that dress anywhere. But she ought to have had a handbag... She did ought to have had a handbag."

"That's a good girl," said the nurse mechanically.

Santonelli, although he knew many more things about the dead woman than Lal Jennings, did not know by the time he led the two Loudens, father and son, down to the police station that Lal had already seen the body and provisionally identified her as her friend Winnie Martin's lodger.

He showed the Loudens a photograph. It was the better of the two photographs. It revealed the shape and size of the woman, it let them see her arms and legs, it showed them the face but shielded them from the worst impact of what mortality had done. "It's Rina," said James Louden to his son.

"It canna be Rina."

"It's Rina, I tell you."

"How do you know?"

"It's got her tiny hands," said James Louden, before he fainted.

129

Chapter 9

SO TWO PEOPLE, Winnie Martin's lodger and Rina Louden of Murreinhead, seemed for the moment to merge.

In both Murreinhead and London this coalescence caused confusion. Coffin was almost inclined to reject the identification.

"I don't think we can set too much store by either of these identifications until one or both have been confirmed," he said. "They've been offered us, that's all; we don't have to take them. Lal Jennings never actually *saw* the woman she claims to identify, she just has a picture and a verbal description to go on and the man Louden has only seen a photograph he thinks is his wife."

Dove studied his fingernails, which had lately developed little white dots; he was quite sure it indicated a sinister degeneration of his health. There had been no other symptoms, though. This did not cheer him up. He just began to worry about what was waiting for him round the corner.

"Louden's coming down to look," went on his boss.

"So he is, so he is." Dove did not raise his eyes from his nails.

"And we're trying to get in touch with Mrs Winnie Martin herself

"So we are." What was this sinister condition hanging over him? Dove hastily ran over everything that was possible. Rheumatism, hypertension, some glandular deficiency? All seemed possible, none absolutely inevitable. This was one of the things that troubled Dove most: that his ill health always seemed impending, yet never arrived. He was actually in splendid health and ate and slept well. Naturally he never included hypochondria among the ailments that threatened. Twenty-four Dove relations were at that moment attending outpatients' clinics and surgeries at hospitals in the district. Ill health was their hobby. "The hot weather's still hanging on, isn't it?" Perhaps it was the heat that was affecting his nails. He tapped them on the table to see if they felt brittle. "The trouble is, Lal Jennings didn't really know her friend's address."

"Was she telling the truth about that, do you think?"

"Oh, yes. There she is, shut up in this house, has been for twenty odd years, and entirely dependent on the friend visiting her. Which the friend did. But the address she has is twenty years out of date. She didn't know that Basso Street was knocked down eight years ago.

"So where *is* Mrs Winnie Martin?"

Coffin shrugged. "She'll turn up. We'll find her or she'll find us. But not in Basso Street."

Lal Jennings was furious with Winnie now that she knew about Basso Street. The police had taken Winnie's address and then told her that Basso Street had been demolished to make way for huge blocks of flats.

Perhaps Winnie Martin lived in one of these flats, they had suggested very politely. But Lal had rejected that vigorously. Winnie had not lived in a flat.

Winnie had lived in a house. She had had her own house and kept it a secret.

"I'll tell that Winnie something when I see her again," said Lal. In her heart, though, she understood the mixture of laziness and secretiveness that had kept Winnie Martin from explaining about Basso Street. "She must have moved about eight years ago. Yes, that must be the time she got the new coal-bin, that'll be why she got it. Wonder where she moved to?" questioned Lal. "Leopold Street? Albany Grove? Lots of little houses like Winnie's round there." But were there? Her memories were twenty years old. Did the world she remembered still exist? She saw now that Winnie, although she had indeed been the means by which the outside world had got through to Lal, had been a severely censored source. There had been a lot Winnie had left unsaid. Things she had not thought worth mentioning and others, which she had downright repressed. "Winnie Martin, you ought to get yourself into trouble."

The relationship between them went back to their childhood, when they had played hopscotch together in the gutters of the Borough, wearing full skirts and petticoats and shiny black boots. During the years the friendship between them had been like a seesaw: sometimes one was in the ascendant, sometimes the other. In the beginning Lal had been the strong prosperous one with the big hearty laugh, and Winnie had been her servant. As Lal's father was a local publican and Winnie's mother had cleaned the bar, Winnie had at one time been literally her servant, and had washed her clothes and polished her boots. There was still this element of service in her relationship with Lal. But the end of the seesaw with Lal on it had gone down and Winnie had gone up. Lal's father had died, and it was Winnie who married the new proprietor and became 'the Missus'. The bomb which crippled Lal killed Winnie's husband in circumstances which allowed Winnie to ask why they were together but not to know for sure. From then on Winnie attended on Lal but kept her secrets. Still, they were two ageing women together. They could not divide themselves from their past, so it shaped their present. Their friendship had survived jealousy, poverty and war.

A great sense of unease slowly filled her.

In Murreinhead, Sergeant Santonelli let Giles know about the tentative identification of Rina Louden with the woman in Creevey Buildings, South London. Giles did not believe it.

"I'm going south with the pair of them," said the sergeant. "Taking the boy and his father."

"They probably want a free trip to London."

"Now that's not the way you ought to talk," said

Santonelli reprovingly. "How are you?"

"Better," said Giles, obscurely disturbed. "Well, let me know if you get a positive identification. I shall have to draw a thick black line under the plea in the court records."

"That'll be her obituary," said Santonelli. Giles thought he sounded thoroughly pleased with himself A country solicitor's office is usually peaceful, perhaps even dull, but Giles had managed to produce a sense of excitement in his which came entirely from his own character. As his staff, one typist and one elderly office girl, often said to each other: "You never can tell what He'll be about next." They always spoke of Giles in capital letters. Giles was He, Him, and Himself. Yet they liked and greatly admired him and promoted his welfare unscrupulously.

Today Giles was an object of particular interest to them as he sat stiffly at his desk. They knew about his wound, of course, all Murreinhead did.

"Were you hurt fending off a robber then, Sir Giles?" Mollie Wishart asked tenderly as she helped Giles to his desk. He didn't need help, resented it even, but he was quite incapable of stopping Mollie, who kept his files, made his tea and bullied the little typist he called his secretary.

"You needn't bother, Mollie, honestly."

"Ach, no bother, a pleasure, Sir Giles." Mollie ruthlessly led him to his chair, on which she had placed a cushion. She was a subtle, grey-haired woman whose diffidence was misleading. When

134

she said to you on any debatable point "Ach, I'm easy, suit yourself," it meant she had made up her mind what should be done and nothing in the world would make her change her mind or act otherwise. Giles knew this now.

"No, it wasn't a robber, Mollie. Or perhaps it was. To tell you the truth, I don't know. Something came up and hit me, I don't remember too much."

"Is it connected with your work for the Burgh Court, Sir Giles, now then do you think?" Mollie never hesitated to let him see that, in her opinion, acting as an official of the court introduced him to a rough, tough world and that he would be better employed in negotiating land sales, arranging marriage settlements and proving wills. Giles had tried to explain to her that hardly anyone had a marriage settlement these days.

"Oh no, I shouldn't think so," he touched the area of his wound gently. It pained him, yet gave him pleasure. He felt, like a Renaissance hero, wounded (in honest combat) but virile. He fancied Mollie Wishart gave a faint smile.

"We've never had anything like it in Murreinhead before."

Giles grinned. "You know better than that, Mollie."

There was another meeting of the Burgh Court today. Giles took it slowly. Out of the corner of his eye he saw that today's meeting was being attended by the reporter from the local paper.

"Thought you usually sent the office-boy," said Giles.

"It's been a girl for years now," said the reporter. "Can't get boys."

"Fleet Street lost its glamour?"

"They call us the Two Minutes' Silence," said the journalist, repeating the old joke with gloomy pleasure. "Still, I came to see you. You're our mystery man, you are."

"No mystery about me."

"You mean you know who did it? Your knifing?"

"No, of course not. If I did, I'd say."

"One of this lot here?" said the reporter, looking round the court, which was filling up.

"I don't think so."

"One of the lot you had here last then?"

Giles turned to study him. "What do you mean?"

"Some tricky cases you had here. The car crash case. Old Agnes Dyke and her boyfriends—not to mention her ghosts..."

"Yes, but still," began Giles.

"Old Lizzie Hamilton is no friend of yours," said the reporter, watching him closely.

Giles smiled, he was fluent in smiles today. "All the same, I don't think old Lizzie stabbed me."

"Oh, you don't?" Now the reporter was really interested. Until now perhaps he had only been playing with Giles; this was a quiet time in Murreinhead, he had come to the Burgh Court meeting out of a mixture of boredom and hope. "So is there some connection with the coat-slashing

136

affair, d'ye think?"

"I suppose there must be," admitted Giles reluctantly. Now it had been put into open speech, he didn't see how it could be denied, but he didn't know what Santonelli was going to say. "But there are none of them here today, you know."

"So I see." His eyes had been searching the court. "Where's Rina Louden?"

Giles was silent.

"You know what lies behind that quarrel, don't you? I mean Lizzie Hamilton and Rina Louden?"

"No."

"If you don't, you must be the only man in Murreinhead who doesn't."

"I dare say."

"Lizzie and Mrs Louden had a stand-up fight. Lizzie doesn't touch a drop, she gets her kicks in other ways, but I dare say Rina Louden might have been drunk."

"Go on."

"Stories differ as to what it was all about—some say Lizzie just picked a quarrel, others say it was because Rina tried to be too friendly with Lizzie's husband."

"I've always thought she beat him," said Giles.

"It was Rina she beat this time. But in return Rina tore a sleeve out of Lizzie's coat. And Lizzie was angry. You know Lizzie."

"Then Lizzie did slash Mrs Louden's coat," said Giles. Somehow, he had never believed it before.

"It looks as though she must have, doesn't it?"

137

"She says she didn't."

"What do you expect? Rina brought it to court."

"It's funny—but I've never caught Lizzie telling a lie."

"Oh, she's a bold woman all right."

"And what about the Louden boy? You were there that day in court, you saw him stand up. What do you make of him? Doesn't it strike you there's questions there to be asked?"

"The question I'd like to ask is what's Lizzie Hamilton doing with a *dog's leash*? I'd like to ask it right out to her face. Lizzie, I'd say, why did you buy that great piece of leather? You haven't got a dog."

All through that long day which seemed longer and warmer than ever Giles debated the question of the boy. Somehow he didn't mind whether Lizzie Hamilton had a dog's leash or not. Lizzie could get on with it.

Giles's face revealed what a beating he had taken, even though his eyes were bright and his manner cheerful. The magistrate was the silent Mr McGinn today. Giles, needing conversation, would have preferred Daniel Blair. William Tulloch was also present but Catriona was not. She was away competing in a Ladies' Golf Championship, which she was sure to win. Catriona won everything. The lines on Giles's face were deeper today, and this too was part of Catriona's prize. He had spent quite a sleepless night looking forward to seeing her, and now she was not here. His sleepless night had included worry and doubts as well as anticipation. He felt as though he, his house and his life were all in the melting pot and might be poured out, quite soon, into a completely different mould. It might not be one he had chosen either. Or would have chosen if a free choice had existed. You were supposed to hate this kind of thing, and perhaps, when the cooling down process had begun, he would hate it, but at the moment, while still boiling up, he felt on the whole exultant. Still, the lines on his face and the faint bruise at the temple where he had struck himself against the wall showed up clearly. He was ageing, no doubt of that. Mr McGinn nodded his head and the next case came on. It seemed a day saved up for dull cases. Small debtors, petty offenders and the town drunk appeared in procession. Jamie was a familiar figure to everyone and there was nothing in the least romantic or interesting about his drinking. He drank when he had the money for it and that was the end of it. These days, fortunately, he had the money less and less often. People said he was better tempered when he was drunk: he was certainly bad-tempered when he was sober.

He scowled at Giles and turned his face away to look out of the window.

"Fine as usual," said Mr McGinn.

"That's no' a sentence," said Jamie. "Mr Blair always says a few words."

"Pay the fine or go to prison," said Mr McGinn, adding his few words.

139

"That's no' what I mean. He tells me something about myself," said Jamie who appeared to have a well-developed streak of masochism. Perhaps he only gets drunk to hear a few words about himself, thought Giles.

"Be off," said McGinn.

Agnes Dyke had appeared at the back of the court. She was wearing a green tweed coat and skirt, with a spray of flowers in the lapel of the jacket. She looks like a bride, thought Giles. This did not apply to her face, however, where her dark eyes glittered.

Alexander Knowles had already arrived and was sitting well to the front. Agnes walked forward and sat next to him. Alexander started to fidget a little, but he did not look at Agnes. Alex Knowles had asked to have the case brought forward to this meeting of the Court. Between this meeting and the last there had been a generous reconsideration of the case. The generosity had not come from Sergeant Santonelli, who remained angry with all the characters concerned, but had sprung from a strong desire on the part of all the local dignitaries to get the case buried before Agnes's ghosts became a national joke. Murreinhead had no desire to find itself lined up with the Loch Ness Monster. Perhaps they were taking it too seriously. What was a ghost, more or less? Some people, like Daniel Blair, thought it might bring trade to the town.

Agnes Dyke's eyes were brilliant as she answered her name. Unlike the last time, she was silent and not shouting. Sergeant Santonelli was not present, because he was away taking the two Loudens to London. Agnes seemed to miss him; she looked round the room as if seeking him. It was true that in the past she had appeared to enjoy, in her way, the sergeant's company. It was this which had alarmed the sergeant so.

"Agnes likes men," he had said gloomily.

As a result of the reconsideration of the case, a sympathetic suggestion had been made to Alex Knowles that he should drop the case, and he had agreed. With relief, some thought.

"I am informed that Mr Knowles withdraws his charges against you, Miss Dyke," said the Magistrate. "And you are therefore discharged."

"I was never in custody," proclaimed Agnes loudly. "Who says so tells a lie."

"From answering only," explained Mr McGinn, closing his eyes.

"I'll answer," said Agnes loudly. "Of course I'll answer. I always answer. Who says I dinna?" She tossed her head.

Who indeed, thought Giles.

"You do not need to answer the charge," said Mr McGinn, opening his eyes again. No doubt he felt, and wisely, it was better to see what Agnes was up to. "There is no charge."

"There is, there is," cried Agnes. "I make one."

"Case dismissed," said Mr McGinn, ignoring her. "Next case, please, Mr Clerk."

"I accuse Alexander Knowles," began Agnes

loudly. An usher came hurriedly over and started to quieten her. She was persuaded to leave. But not before Giles had heard the ominous word 'ghosts'. Agnes was away again.

After Agnes's rapid but stimulating appearance the day seemed to drag. Giles used the monotony to think his own thoughts. This ability (more obvious to others than Giles realised) to meditate while apparently engaged in business, was one of the qualities which made Willie Tulloch ask himself if Giles was really well suited to his profession. "He should start at the top and be a Judge. There it would suit admirably," Willie had pronounced, rolling his r's. "But at the bottom ranks of the profession..." and he spread his hands wide. Willie could be quite an actor. "A man wants to be sure it's his feu duty and rents his lawyer is thinking about when he says 'Um' and not the five orders of architecture." (Willie naturally favoured the Doric himself.)

What about the boy? Giles was asking himself Where does he come in? Why does he worry me? And who has been hitting him?

The obvious answer to this was his parents, one or other of them. But why?

Did they have a case of ill treatment of a minor here? And did Giles have a duty to report it to anyone? The boy looked strong and wiry, well able (you would have said) to defend himself. But at the same time, adults often had the upper hand emotionally. Somewhere in this case Giles could

142

feel powerful emotions welling up.

The luncheon gathering that day was a dull one; the only ones present were Giles and Mr McGinn, who did not speak throughout the meal, but bent his head towards his soup and then his lamb cutlet. Giles had thought of taking in his friend the journalist but by the end of the morning he too had disappeared.

But Mr McGinn did not remain entirely silent. After he had finished his cheese oatcake and allowed a full minute of silence for digestion, he cleared his throat.

Giles recognised the preamble to conversation and looked up expectantly.

Mr McGinn picked up an apple, considered eating it, then put it down. He cleared his throat again. There was no nervousness in this habit (although it frequently made other people nervous), it was simply his method of beginning to speak. He must have learnt it as a baby, thought Giles, and never been able to give it up. At once he had a vivid picture of an elderly Mr McGinn sitting in a high chair, waving a rattle and clearing his throat. "You will be wondering, perhaps," he began, "why I have taken such an interest in the car crash case."

"Oh no," said Giles politely, meaning really of course, oh yes. "Oh, I'm sorry, I'm afraid your apple has rolled off the table."

"It wasn't such a good one anyway," said Mr McGinn, letting Giles pick it up. "There's no such thing as a good apple these days. For eating, that

143

is. I know nothing about cooking. They all come from Italy or California or South Africa," he said with contempt.

"It's not too bad," said Giles, who was eating it.

"The truth is, I suspect, there was bad management over the car crash," Mr McGinn had resumed his subject. "Bad management. Who told the police about the crash? What was this business about an anonymous phone call? There was someone else present, you know."

"I remember thinking that myself," said Giles.

"So you might, so you might."

"Someone who hasn't come forward?"

"Aye."

Giles put down the apple on the plate. "Does it make any real difference?" He was thinking of the young defendant, Peter Robert Bell, and his despairing beaten face. "Aye, but it does," said Mr McGinn slowly. "It's a matter of insurance, d'ye see."

Giles did see.

"It makes a little query. Insurance companies are just not going to like that."

"Money, money." said Giles.

"Aye, money talks," answered Mr McGinn. "It may only whisper but people hear it and listen."

"There's always gossip," said Giles.

"So there is, so there is."

They sat in silence for a minute. Then: "I might as well tell you, since we're being confidential," murmured Mr McGinn, "that they're saying all over the town that you stabbed yourself "

"It's strange," said John Coffin aloud and yet also to his own private ear, "about this dead woman. We've had two people offer identification, both different. They could both turn out to be right."

"I suppose so," said Dove, making it sound doubtful. He never disagreed with his superior, but he never quite agreed either.

"And yet we don't really know anything about her," said Coffin, pursuing his own thoughts.

"We'll know more when the husband gets here," said Dove soothingly. "if he is her husband."

This time Dove remained quiet.

"We need to see the landlady, Mrs Martin. Where is she? Why is she always out when we call?"

They had found out where Winnie Martin lived now. She had a small house in Pompey Street, not far from Cato Docks. She had not moved far from Basso Street. The policeman on the beat knew her quite well and had reported her address. "Nice old girl," he had said. "Difficult to get to know, though. Keeps herself to herself."

"Well, she can't help it," said Dove, as if trying to be reasonable.

"Can't she? Can't she?" Coffin stopped his prowling round the room and stood still. "Why can't she?"

Sergeant Dove stared at him.

"Perhaps that's the question we ought to be asking?" said Coffin softly. "Why can't she help it?"

The bell was on the door in Pompey Street and the door was locked, but what was behind the door?

Chapter 10

WITHIN THE NEXT few hours the police were back at Winnie Martin's house. Coffin and Dove stood outside, staring at the facade; they were accompanied by two police constables. They were there in force, and with a fixed intention.

"Don't want to break the front door down," murmured Coffin. "Alarm the neighbours."

"They're watching already," said Dove, whose professional eye had caught a twitch of curtain, and a movement from behind a window box.

"Of course." Coffin was brisk. "Saw us arrive. Still, we don't want to give them too much excitement."

"That's old Mrs Tiger up there," said Dove. "Her behind the window-box. Can't mistake that stance. Looks like a boxer. I'd know her anywhere. Heard she'd moved round here."

"*Tiger?*" said Coffin. He was used to unlikely names among the inhabitants of his district, but this name was still remarkable.

"Yes, you know, sir. She's the widow of old Tiger Thomas who took the Featherweight European Championship off the coloured boys three times in a row. They say she trained him herself."

"She looks as though she could have gone into the ring with him," said Coffin, observing the stalwart figure only partly obscured by the geraniums. "Wonder how Tiger would have liked that?"

"'Oh, she was twice his weight."

"Who's that with her?"

Dove hesitated to answer. Possibly he didn't know.

"That's young Mrs Tiger," said one of the constables.

"Two of them?" exclaimed Coffin incredulously.

"The son's wife. He took his father's name and tried his luck in the ring, but it didn't come to anything. Drink, sir," explained the constable. The other constable laughed; the two young men seemed very friendly with each other. "Not a patch on his old man."

"And where is he now?" "I think that's him behind the two women, sir. Terrible gossip he is these days—See All and Hear All, we call his wife and him."

"I'll remember that," said Coffin. "It might come in useful. Can we get in round the back?"

"Not unless we climb the wall. But I've got a key, sir."

"You have?"

"It's quite easy to come by a key from this street, sir. One key fits the lot."

"I hope you haven't spread that knowledge," cried Coffin.

"It's quite widely known, sir," he was a calm, large young man of unruffled competence. As he looked at him, Coffin had the uneasy feeling that someone was walking on his grave. I am looking at my successor, he felt. When I am an old man, creeping

148

around in my retirement, *he* will be ruling in my manor. Their eyes met. And damn it, thought Coffin, he knows it. It is what he *intends*.

"How old are you?" he asked suddenly.

"Twenty-five, sir." The constable looked surprised, even alarmed. Perhaps his ambitions and hopes had shown more clearly than he realised. Or perhaps Coffin was being over-imaginative.

Side by side they went towards Winnie Martin's front door. A neat little card with the word 'Ring twice for Martin' was pinned below the bell.

Coffin rang twice. There was no answer.

Dove pressed his shoulder against the door. It gave slightly at top and bottom.

"Only locked," he said. "Not bolted."

"What did you expect?" Coffin looked round. "Give me the key."

The door opened easily.

"Why 'Ring twice for Martin', I wonder?" he said, looking round. "The lodger, I suppose. One ring only for the lodger. Did the lodger get many visitors then?"

"It's sort of the custom round here," put in the constable. "Winnie wouldn't give the lodger a key, but she'd let the lodger and her visitors have a special ring on the door."

"Strangers keep out, in other words?"

The young policeman shrugged. "They're funny round here. If they don't feel like opening the door, they don't. Goes back to the war. I think. Half the boys were deserters from the army and in hiding."

They filed into the hall and stood silent.

There was something about the little house that compelled silence. A fly buzzing on the window was the only sound. It flew under Coffin's nose and he swatted at it.

"Kill that thing," he said in sudden anger.

The fly got away with no difficulty. There was complete silence now, no ticking clock, no dripping taps. A house where people are living and moving around is always settling itself down with minute creaks and rustles. Here was a heavy dullness. The policemen had startled the fly into movement. Otherwise nothing had moved in this house for a long time.

"Well, get on with it," said Coffin. "We know what to do, don't we?"

The young policeman started to cough.

"Yes. It does smell rather," said Coffin. "We won't have to look far," he walked forward to the sitting room. A foot in a brown shoe poked out from behind the door. "No farther than here."

When Lal Jennings realised that Basso Street was really gone, she could hardly contain herself It had taken her some time to grasp exactly how misleading Winnie had been.

"Basso Street clean gone," muttered Lal. "Old Basso Street doesn't exist any more. I can't believe it. All these years I've had the picture in my mind of things as they were, as they used to be, and it's

150

not true. All gone. Been gone for years. Half the things I talked about and pictured just weren't there." She grappled with the enormity of it. "Basso Street, the dairy at the corner where they used to sell milk straight into your jug, old Mrs Keats, the midwife, at number five, all gone."

"You don't want to brood on it," said her home help briskly. She was bringing in the supper tray. "Old Mrs Keats would be over ninety if she was still alive."

"When did she go?" asked Lal ghoulishly.

"Don't *brood* on it, dear. It's better to think that you've got it all straight now." Privately, she wondered how it was that Lal hadn't started getting it straight ages ago. Of course, a district didn't stand still. Things changed, developed, all the time. The opposite was petrifaction. "You should have asked me more, dear. I could have set you straight ages ago."

Lal stared at her without answering. What she said seemed without meaning. Never had the gulf between them been wider.

"It's not a question of setting me straight," she grumbled. "I've been living in a world that didn't exist. I can't get my feet. I'm lost, can't you understand that ?"

"Mrs Martin certainly misled you. Drink that milk, there's a good girl. Here's your toast." She withdrew her hand rapidly as Lal's teeth snapped down on a piece of toast. Surely Miss Jennings wouldn't try to *bite* her?

151

"You couldn't call it misleading," brooded Lal.

"No? Not misleading?"

"Ah, no," said Lal almost indulgently. The relationship between her and Winnie Martin had gone on too long for her to be able to separate herself entirely from Winnie yet. She understood why Winnie had let it go on. She had kept Lal in a dream world because she wanted to be in it herself. When she talked about it to Lal they both lived in it. Basso Street and its environs was their old world that was dead.

Poor Winnie, how lonely and frightened she must, have been, thought Lal, who had always believed herself the stronger character, not entirely seeing that clearly among Winnie's motives had been the impulse to hold Lal in check. Lal was Winnie's prisoner, her mind and body equally tethered. Impossible not to believe that Winnie had known this and enjoyed it.

The home help saw this and quite enjoyed the thought. "She was just having you on," she said briskly.

"Perhaps she was trying to protect me." And Lal shivered a little, dreading to feel the cold wind blowing from this new hard world she was living in so surprisingly. "Poor Winnie. So silly, so silly." She was sure she was the stronger one now. "So trusting."

"Is that what you call it?" The woman brought over Lal's bowl of fruit and nervously held out an orange. The strange expression on Lal's face made her wonder if Miss Jennings was indeed capable of biting the hand that fed her. "You'll have to give her a word of warning, she said with heavy irony.

Lal turned her head away; it was her only way of escape.

"We shall never see her again."

"Oh, she'll come back, dear."

"She's dead." Lal turned her head round and stared. Her eyes were full of tears. "Can't you work that out for yourself? Dead."

The home help stood and stared at her, her hands hanging by her sides. She couldn't speak.

"And what I'm asking myself is: did the lodger kill her and then herself? Or did someone kill them both?"

"If you think that you ought to tell the police." She just stopped herself saying "Go to the police," but of course Lal couldn't go anywhere unless you took her. She herself was hurriedly taking off her overall and preparing to depart; she was nervous. She had some queer people to look after in other homes. There was old Mrs Moss who had a spittoon (and used it) and Elfrida Dove who said the birds spoke to her. (And the things they said made one wonder about the private lives of birds.) But Lal Jennings frightened her. She was unnerving. At this moment her hands were clasping and unclasping themselves.

"Winnie had something on her mind last time I saw her," said Lal. "She knew something. Something she'd seen or something she'd heard.

She thought she'd covered it up so I wouldn't know, but I did know. She could never hide much from me. ' And to tell you the truth, I've thought about it a lot since then. What did Winnie know?"

"What was there for Winnie to know?" said the other woman helplessly.

"I dunno," said Lal. "I dunno."

The body of Winnie Martin lay on the floor in her own sitting room and they were all staring at it. She lay on her face just as she had fallen, with one knee drawn up and one leg cocked out, somewhat at an angle.

She had been dead a few weeks, but strangely enough her body was better preserved than the other dead woman's had been. Something in the atmosphere of the house, hot as the weather had been, had only shrivelled her, not destroyed her. Winnie was a little smaller, a little more wizened, but recognisably herself.

Coffin moved round the room. In a few minutes the police technicians would have arrived and the body would be photographed, measured, and fingerprinted. But just now it was still as it had been on the last day Winnie Martin had lived in it.

A strange little woman. Coffin thought. You could read Winnie's character in her house, but you had to read carefully. Winnie seemed to have brought everything she owned with her from Basso Street. Books, pictures, furniture and clothes were all crammed into the room. No doubt there was just as much in other rooms too. It was all Winnie's past. There was an armchair by the window with a table next to it and this was clearly where Winnie had sat, looking out. A folded newspaper rested on the seat.

He picked it up and observed the date.

"She was probably killed on the same day as the other woman. I wonder which went first?"

There was a photograph of Lal Jennings with long curly hair, and wearing a flowered silk dress. Her hair had been black and crisp in those days. Coffin picked it up and studied it. In the background of the picture was a tall, heavy man. Winnie had some of Lal's past in this room too as well as her own.

Coffin had interviewed Lal and found her a puzzle. "You know, I've got the distinct impression that she needn't be a cripple if she didn't choose," he had said to Dove.

"Really?" Naturally this was a subject which interested Dove. "Hysterical, you mean." No one had ever looked less hysterical than Lal.

"I'm not sure. Emotional is a better word, possibly," said Coffin thoughtfully. Surely no one had ever seemed *less* emotional than Lal?

"She got too close to the murderer," said Coffin, looking down on Winnie. "She was in the way, somehow. Was that why she was killed, Dove?"

"There's certainly a clear link between the dead woman in Creevey Buildings and Winnie Martin and Winnie Martin's lodger. The dead woman and

155

the lodger must be the same person."

"If so, then there will be fingerprints to match."

"And we still won't be much forwarder." Dove was always gloomy, except when his superior was, and then he felt it his duty (or his pleasure) to be cheerful.

"I'm not so sure."

There was a noise from the next room. It was a quiet enough noise, the sound of something falling.

The young policeman appeared at the door. He had a strange, half startled, half-amused look on his face.

"We're not deaf," said Coffin.

"Something funny in there, sir," he nodded towards the next room; there was a suppressed excitement, even amusement, in his voice. He stood aside to let his seniors pass. "It was the tenant's room, sir, I guess."

"What are you looking so pleased about?"

"Not pleased, sir."

"You're a jump ahead of me."

"Time, they say, is a fourth dimension, sir."

Coffin looked tired. This young man was ageing him perceptibly, minute by minute.

"Show us what you've got."

The room next door had been got up in a makeshift kind of way as a bed-sitting room. That is to say, there was a bed and there were chairs. Apart from a table and a cupboard there was little else. Apparently it had never been prepared for anyone to live in it. Probably Winnie Martin had never planned to let the room.

Signs of habitation were few, no clothes, no possessions, hardly anything except an imperceptible disarrangement that spoke of someone living there.

In one corner, close by the window, was a big old cupboard made of some unidentifiable dark wood. The door of this cupboard was open; the top two shelves were jammed full of handbags. Some had fallen to the ground. "That was what you heard falling," said the young policeman.

Coffin picked up one handbag. The handle had been cut off, as if with a knife. Another on the floor had been slashed. Every bag there had been savaged.

There were fingerprints in the room.

"Not so many as you'd expect," said Coffin. "Perhaps someone has been trying to wipe them out."

These fingerprints were soon matched up and shown to be identical with those of the victim in Creevey Buildings.

"So she did live here, or come here anyway," said Coffin; he had always been doubtful. "Who camped out in the Buildings then? Perhaps no one did, perhaps it was just a bolt-hole." In that squalid room in Creevey Buildings no fingerprints that could be used had been found.

In addition to the fingerprints of the victim, a

few unidentified prints had been found. These did not belong to Winnie Martin or the dead woman in Creevey Buildings. In any case they were not those of a woman, but appeared to be those of a man. These prints were found on only one object, a small leather case which had held a watch. Because the police were efficient and methodical and painstaking this second set of prints was compared with those on the knife which Sergeant Santonelli had sent down to London.

The prints matched. The hand that had held the knife which had dug into Giles Almond in Murreinhead had also left impressions of itself in London. The prints themselves could not yet be given a name.

The positive identification of the dead woman in Creevey Buildings with Rina Louden followed within a matter of hours.

On his way home that night, tired, but deeply absorbed and interested in the case, John Coffin passed the young policeman. His friend was still with him.

Out working late and as bright as a bird, thought Coffin. He had a sudden remembrance of himself twenty years ago. I have a past now, he thought, and perhaps it's already bigger than my future.

"Are you married?" he asked.

"Yes, sir."

"Any children?"

"Twin sons, sir."

"Don't they tire you out?" said Coffin.

"Away at school, sir."

"They are?" Coffin was startled. "You must have married young."

"We do, sir, in my walk of life," he answered apologetically.

Coffin gave him a suspicious look and walked on.

As he got into his car, the other young constable whispered. "He's a lord, sir."

"What? Go on, he can't be," said Coffin irritably.

"They say so, sir. Doesn't use his title, of course. They say he's only doing it to get experience of life. Going into politics, they say."

"Rubbish." Coffin could not approve of a policeman with a peerage, democratic or otherwise. He got into his car.

As he drove away, he recalled that eager face. "He won't be content with my manor. He's aiming at the Cabinet. Damn it, in twenty years time I will probably be hobbling into Madame Tussaud's and saying: yes, that's him. I used to know the Prime Minister."

Coffin stood outside his own house for a moment and breathed in the night air. Even in London the night air smelt sweeter and softer than the day air. Tonight the compound of smoke, dust and oil, together with a special something that was London's alone, smelt especially fragrant to him. The heat still held, but a break was coming. He could feel it. As he stood there, a few drops of rain fell on his face, and then a few more. Within ten minutes it was raining heavily.

In the gutters of Sweetwater Street, not far from Creevey Buildings and near to the police station, the rainwater was soon flowing merrily, rather like the small spring which had once run there in seventeenth century London, and from which the street took its name. The water eddied and swirled round a small object which glinted there.

The water wasn't going to do it much good. In spite of all the improvements of science, water is still not good for watches.

Chapter 11

JAMES LOUDEN and his son Joseph were sitting in sullen exhausted silence in a café at King's Cross. They were on their way home, and they were not pleased with each other.

"I like the other way home best," said the boy.

"What do you know about that?" His father was sharp.

"Ha."

"Nothing you ought to know."

"Nothing I ought to know and everything I do know."

"You keep quiet."

"Well, the police won't, that's sure. D'ye think they're not asking themselves how Rina got down here. She didn't have wings you know, not our Rina," he gave a laugh.

"She's gone. Don't talk about her like that."

The boy was silent. The force and energy of Rina alive still hung over him; he could not believe she was really gone.

"All that business of the coat," he said. "Nothing'll come of it now."

"It was never important."

"No," said the boy, more doubtfully than his father. But then his father had never known much of the story. It was really quite important. "Do you think the police will come and ask us any more questions? The London Police. I mean?"

"They're bound to, aren't they? They can't leave

it. They're letting us have it easy at the moment. But they'll be back."

"Yes." No one had asked him any questions yet, but no doubt his father was right, questions were on the way. "I haven't got anything to tell them."

"Everyone always says that. You, me, everyone, but the police get at 'em just the same."

It was borne in upon the boy that James Louden was frightened. Very frightened. He looked at him with interest, not unmixed with relief. It seemed more human somehow for his father to be frightened. He had always up to this time had the uneasy feeling that his father might not be quite human. Godlike, more. An irritable, omniscient, possessive god. You didn't want a jealous deity for a father. Especially when you'd got Rina for a mother.

"You're not the same as everyone," he said, dragging out unwillingly the deep truth he had always believed. His father was not the same as everyone. Rina was the same as everyone, only more so. He himself, born of them, was probably unique. It was a heavy burden, being unique.

"I dinna ken what you're talking about." His father's speech (and usually he spoke carefully and well, as if he liked the sound of his own voice) was getting slovenly as he grew tireder and colder. He shivered. "I'll be glad to get out of here."

"Let's go the other way," said the boy, leaning forward and speaking softly. "There's still time... we could pick 'em up at Market Cross."

162

"What's the good?"

"We could go out and never come back."

"Look, Sergeant Santonelli brought us down here. He's gone back home. But he's waiting for us. He'll be looking for us there. And if we don't turn up, he'll be looking for us here."

"We needn't be here. We could go anywhere, anywhere in the world. A man like you knows the way," he was speaking again to the god. Hoping this time, as so often with the worshipper, to exploit the godhead. You give: I'll take.

"Keep your voice down."

"We'll go then? We'll go off?" He was starting to rise to his feet. "Market Cross."

"You use Market Cross, do you?" His father was still sitting there. "And how do you know how to find what you're looking for?"

"Oh, I go for the lorry parked under the trees. It's always parked under the trees near the lavatory. Every Tuesday around nine at night, or if not Tuesday the next night."

"Or wait till the next week?"

"Oh, I've never had that happen. It's as regular as a bus service." His voice was confident. "And if it's not there, you can always tout around and perhaps pick up another one. I mean, there's always one."

"Do you ever do that?"

"Once or twice," he was beginning, and against his will, to be excited. "We do them a service really, riding in their beaten-down old lorries. Anyway they like us. It's got to be a sort of habit. For them and us. And all the people that travel that way."

They both had access to a sub-world. If you knew the ropes you could always get a lift north along the lorry routes. You had to know the right places to wait and the right way to climb aboard. It was a world with its own laws and its own respectabilities. Its own risks too. Not everyone who used the route' had nice manners. But once you had a free pass into this world you could travel anonymously and fast. They could both drop into this sub-world and disappear forever. Without Rina.

"Shall we go then?" He was very eager.

"No."

"No? But you said..."

"I didn't say anything. I just wanted to know how much Rina had taught you."

"You only asked me so you could find out what I knew." Disappointment flooded into his voice. "But it's a good idea, what I'm saying. We can go." They could run. But Rina might come too.

"No." His father pushed him back into his chair.

"Why not?"

"I owe it to Rina," he spoke judicially, as if his mind was weighed up. "I owe it to Rina. She was a good sort, Rina. She wasn't fit to be a mother, but she was a good sort

"You didn't always say that."

The ghost of Rina was pushing between them.

"I loved Rina."

"I suppose she *was* your wife?"

"That's a fine thing for *you* to say."

"I don't think you know how I felt about Rina, Dad."

"No, I don't think I do."

"I can't really believe she's dead," he whispered. "But you did kill her, didn't you?"

Chapter 12

NEITHER JOHN COFFIN nor Sergeant Santonelli of Murreinhead believed in omens. Nevertheless each that day was glad to welcome one, and neither called it that, of course.

To John Coffin, the watch which had been picked up out of the rain-filled gutter by the two young policemen on their way home was a complication. Its number and markings showed it to be the watch already, as he knew from Santonelli, associated with Rina Louden, perhaps even stolen by her; and now it had appeared in a gutter in his manor. It hadn't been there yesterday or even long today. The case was unscratched and still polished and it was ticking. True, it didn't need winding up, and would tick on forever, given an occasional odd movement to wind up the sophisticated mechanism. It was magic. But even a magic watch wouldn't tick on if filled with London grime or stepped on by heavy city feet. But the real miracle was, as Coffin pointed out to himself, that it was picked up by a policeman and not by any of those eager hands which would so readily have pocketed it and sold it. The watch could have turned up weeks later in a pawnshop. He almost wished it had.

"You're a complication," he said, holding it up and studying it, on the morning after it was found. "Because you tie Rina Louden's death, and Winnie Martin's also, much closer to Murreinhead than I expected."

Yesterday, he and Dove had accepted the idea that the murderer and bag slasher was a local. That being so, it was only a matter of time before he was located.

"Check on our list of all men who've been convicted or seriously suspected of attacks on women or of any sexual offences. Check on all new comedians coming in from elsewhere."

A 'comedian' was a man who made strange noises, who made 'a joke'. Perhaps he liked wearing woman's clothes or make-up. Perhaps he collected milk bottles, perhaps he believed he was a bat; they'd had all of them in Coffin's district.

"Or a character actor."

A 'character actor' was a man with a false front; someone pretending very hard to be what he was not. Most confidence men were character actors. But plenty of 'character actors' were men whose true faces were twisted.

"Check on those, and ten to one we'll have the killer." Coffin had spoken with confidence. In his mind he was already running over the list. There was 'Fisherman' Jones who had just come out of prison and who had never shown violence before but was said by the doctors to be capable of it. Then there was Big Tod O'Connor who was four feet high with enormous biceps and a wicked temper. He could climb too. Also there was Felix, who hung around the railway stations and tried to steal suitcases. He only liked red cases. Perhaps he had turned his attention to handbags.

True, none of these had been known to associate with Rina Louden, but Coffin had been hopeful.

But with the appearance of the watch, positively identified by Santonelli as the one which had first introduced him to James Louden, the whole country seemed wide open.

Santonelli was delighted when the watch turned up again. It introduced something he could comprehend into a case he had found bewildering. A stolen watch was something he could understand and believe in. "It's interesting about the watch," he said, not realising he was saluting a hope rather than a fact. The watch itself was neither important nor interesting, but its appearance did something to the way both Coffin and Santonelli were thinking.

At first Coffin had been disconcerted and puzzled by its appearance. He didn't like it. But in a very few minutes he saw that the fingerprints on the leather watchcase, the prints on the knife and the ownership of the watch and indeed the personality of Rina Louden herself could all be put together and a whole picture made of them.

It was so simple it hurt.

He picked up the telephone to speak to Sergeant Santonelli.

At the centre of every murder case is the person who is closest to the heart of the victim. The nearest one emotionally, whether it is love or hate. (The two often seem interchangeable.) This person is not necessarily the next of kin.

"Can you get me James Louden, Santonelli? Prints, the whole build up. I'm checking here. It was a mistake to let him go off..." he listened. "Not off the train? Not been seen? You're sure?... No, I see you can't be," he thought for a few minutes. "Right, I'll come up. Have a car to meet me at the airport."

"If Louden's not up there, why are you going then?" asked Dove, who had been listening.

"Someone's up there." Coffin was putting his notes and papers into a little case, and wondering how to let his wife know. She was at the theatre at this moment, and interruptions would not be welcome. "There's someone in the Louden house."

"What about them coping?"

"I want to see, Dove. Just see," said Coffin, still putting his possessions into his leather case, which was now full to bursting. "Call it curiosity if you like."

"You going away for a week?" said Dove, eyeing the case. He wouldn't have minded a trip himself.

Coffin cut short his hope. "Check whether Louden has form."

"He hasn't."

"And he's not a monkey?"

A 'monkey' is a man who has never been in prison, never done time, but is the known associate of criminals. He is a monkey on a stick and it is usually only a matter of time before his stick breaks and he's down there with his friends.

Dove shrugged. "Could be. I can't get it clear.

Perhaps they'll tell you up there. We don't know him down here. I don't think that means anything, though. To tell you the truth, I don't trust him."'

His senior did not answer. No fair answer was possible. He did not trust James Louden either and yet perhaps this was unjust to the man. He was beginning to have an uneasy feeling that James Louden's case, like Rina's, was outside the scope of words like fairness and justice.

"I'll just have a look see," he said finally, reverting to the slang of his childhood. He looked more cheerful. "I've never been to Scotland, you know."

In Murreinhead the day's meeting of the Burgh Court was just over. No rain had fallen in the north yet but it was prophesied. Meanwhile the day was grey and sultry.

Giles followed William Tulloch out of the courtroom. He had behind him a full day's work. He hoped he looked cooler, cleverer, and more in control than he felt.

"Well, I'm glad we got to the bottom of that," said James McGinn, rubbing his hands. "Just as well we didn't have Lady Rose present," he and Daniel Blair had both been sitting today. Lady Rose Rayburn... Rabbie's Irish Rose as she was known locally... had once again excused herself from her place on the rota because of ill health. Ill health often overcame her at this season of the year when there was a good deal going on in London. She had a granddaughter coming out, and a goddaughter on the point of contracting a marriage so grand it was very nearly an alliance, and Lady Rose, sick, but nimble and ready for enjoyment, meant to be present and wearing her best hat. One of the sayings credited to her in the town (and much enjoyed, really) was 'You can't wear a Dior dress in Murreinhead'. Lady Rose, it was presumed, had her wardrobe full of Dior dresses and meant to wear them out. Murreinhead would come in for them when they were more worn, and liked this just as well. They were proud of Lady Rose. But she would have gone poking her nose into the case of the day, and wanting to rum up things that were better left untouched.

It was the car crash case which James McGinn was talking about. In court today the young man accused of causing the accident, Peter Bell, had appeared with his lawyer. There was a mild stir of surprise at their appearance. It was a very mild stir, however; Murreinhead had almost forgotten the case. The excitement over Rina Louden being found dead in London and Agnes Dyke having ghosts had obliterated everything else. So no one except James McGinn and Giles Almond had been excited when the boy appeared and was at last willing to explain what he knew about the telephone call that had summoned the police. There had been a girl with him whom he wanted to protect. She had made the call. Then she had fled. "I'm glad you think we have got to the bottom of it," Giles said.

"Och, for sure." James McGinn looked benevolent and pleased. The insurance company would pay up now.

"I'm not mad about it," muttered Giles.

Willie Tulloch and Catriona came across to them. Giles gave them the wary look of someone who has been made welcome once but is now not quite sure of his reception.

Willie offered him a bow and smile which could mean anything and Catriona, as usual, was giving nothing away. Or was she? Couldn't he see with half an eye that she was looking radiant?

Oh, Catriona, do I love you or fear you? He asked himself with a groan. All the same, he was happy and he too, without knowing it, had an air that matched Catriona's. Nothing would make him handsome, though, and Willie Tulloch, who loved good looks whether in a piece of furniture or a human being, was in despair. You'll never be bonny, lad, he thought, but you could at least be kempt.

Giles jerked at the button on his jacket, unaware that the way it was hanging, half on, half off, was annoying his future father-in-law. "I'm not happy about this crash," Giles said to Catriona. "I'm sure the girl was driving the car."

"I think so, too."

"The boy might go to prison," said Giles wretchedly. The case had been sent up to the Sheriff's Court for trial.

Catriona shrugged. "You did what you could." She was sufficiently her father's daughter to believe that people were what they made themselves. But in her case this belief was fortified by the addition that people were also what their wives made them. She looked at Giles, tender and brilliant, smiled and put her arm through his. "There's Sergeant Santonelli over there," she said with a nod. "And who's that with him?"

But even as they watched, the man with Santonelli had murmured something to the sergeant and turned away. They watched him walk off

Coffin wanted to walk round the town on his own. He had been two hours with Santonelli and seen the town and the Loudens through Santonelli's eyes, now he wanted to see for himself.

"I don't know if anyone's in the house," Santonelli had said. "Something's going on there, but I can't get in."

"Tried?"

"Not too hard," admitted Santonelli. "I haven't knocked the door down or anything like that."

The Louden house did not surprise Coffin. He was expert in shut-up houses. He could almost tell at a glance whether it was an innocent house or a house in which something guilty had been played out or was still being enacted.

"He's in there still," he said at once to himself. "In that room at the front, probably. Been there all the time, I expect."

He ignored the door and went over to the

window and rapped on it. "Come out and let me in," he called.

James Louden appeared at the other side of the window and stared through the glass. He looked flushed, and yet underneath the flush was a great pallor. He stared without expression into Coffin's face.

He knows me all right, thought Coffin. And then, he's been crying.

He left the window and went to stand by the front door. Not to his surprise, it was soon opened by James Louden.

"What do you want?" he asked in a thick voice. "The other one came round but I wouldn't let him in."

"You let me in."

"You're from London. You might have something to say."

"You look ill."

"I've been sick," he said vaguely. "Sick, you know."

"There's a lot of it about."

"Aye."

"Santonelli wasn't sure you'd come back. No one saw you get off the train."

Louden was silent for a long time, then he said: "There's other ways of travelling. You don't have to go by train."

"I know that."

"Of course you do."

"Lorries are the best, of course. But I've heard

you can pick up a boat if you know the ropes. Your wife did know, I suppose?"

"She was a traveller, was Rina." For the first time a livelier note sounded in his voice. It was almost one of appreciation and amusement. Rina had been odd and he knew it. He was odd himself. "Should have been a gypsy. She did have a bit of gypsy blood from her granny. Backwards and forwards between here and London. I don't know how she learnt the ropes. She was doing it when I met her."

"Why did she do it, do you think?" Louden shrugged. "Variety. She was soon bored. Maybe something else as well. I'm not sure."

Coffin thought there *was* something else as well. He did not like the brooding look on the man's face. He looked sick.

"She had some purpose in going to London so often. She took a room there." A room full of handbags, he thought. Had Rina been the person who put those handbags there? Had Rina been the person who rented that room? It couldn't be as simple as that.

"Where's the boy?" he asked.

Louden did not answer immediately, then he said: "He's tired."

"A strange life for him."

"He enjoyed it, I think."

"We found your watch." Coffin was leaning up against the wall just inside the door with Louden between him and the door. He wondered if he had been wise to come here on his own.

"I thought you would. Rina had it."

"I don't know about that."

"We've never found the knife that killed your wife."

"She was stabbed, then?"

Coffin nodded. "But we have another knife. It has a few prints on it, they match the prints on the box belonging to your watch," he was studying Louden's face closely. There was no surprise written on it.

"Will you show me your hand? Palm up."

Silently Coffin looked carefully at each hand, paying particular attention to the fingertips. His eyes traced a diagonal scar, which cut across palm and fingers.

"Nasty cut you had there," he said.

"Not a cut. A rope burn."

Coffin took up Louden's right hand and looked at it again. Finally he said, "I'm no expert, but I would be prepared to bet that your fingerprints match those on the knife."

"I thought they would," said Louden dully. "It's my knife, ye ken."

Coffin nodded. He was listening to the sound of Louden's breathing.

"Wait a minute," said Louden thickly. "Sick. Me."

Coffin nodded.

Louden disappeared behind the nearest door. He was gone a few minutes. Coffin waited. Then he pushed open the door. The room was empty and the window beyond was open.

Not quite the oldest trick in the book, but certainly one that occurred to few within so few bites of the apple. Coffin ran to the window and leaned out. "Come back, you fool," he yelled. "You know I'll get you."

All people knew was that the hunt was up and away from Murreinhead before they even realised it was on, and that the policeman from London who had only just arrived had left before they had had a chance to get to know him. Santonelli thought it might do him a bit of good all the same, and he might get promotion and a move.

"He looked like the sort of man I'd like to know," lamented Giles Almond, who had only seen John Coffin from a distance. "Funny. I thought I knew his face. Perhaps we met in London."

"What was there about London, Giles?" asked Catriona softly. "You've always been hiding something, haven't you?"

Giles hesitated.

"Don't worry then," said Catriona. "If you'd rather not say." She meant to be Giles's wife but she would let him have his secrets. She would keep her own too.

"No, I'll tell you. Anyway, this other business, here in Murreinhead, when I think I was not a coward..."

"No, indeed," said Catriona loyally.

"Has made it all right," went on Giles. "I'll tell

you. It was when I was living in London, when I was trying to be an artist. I do paint quite well, my love. It was a rough part where I lived, but that was part of it, d'you see? I thought I was a big boy. There was a man on the same floor; thin little fellow. We used to talk on the stairs. I don't know what he did. He wasn't an artist, anyway. Worked in a shop, I think. Somehow that made it worse. I mean, if he'd been going to be rich, or famous, but no, this was his life, it was all he had."

"Yes?"

"He got beaten up in the street by a gang of boys. I was too frightened to interfere. I just walked right on. That's all."

"All?"

"It was enough, wasn't it?" said Giles.

In London, in Coffin's district, a doctor was anxiously consulting his records and wondering whether he should consult the police.

"I suppose I'd better," he said to his wife. He was a tall Indian, who was known locally with affection as 'our coloured doctor'. Indian doctors had always done well in that part of the world.

He hadn't helped Rina Louden very much with her problem, though.

Chapter 13

THE HEAT had lifted in London and the epidemic of sickness was waning. Coffin had received the message from the doctor and interviewed him. But by this time what he learnt only confirmed what he already knew.

The hunt was on in London.

"I don't think Louden knows his way around all that much," said Coffin. "We'll soon get him."

"If he comes here. He's a sailor. Take a ship and be off more likely," said Dove. He knew very little about sailors and ships.

"This isn't the eighteenth century," said Coffin. "It's not that easy. He's a worried, frightened man. I think we'll find him."

"He's got plenty to be frightened about."

"Also, he's not clever," went on Coffin. "He'll only have limited ideas."

"And one of them is that he's innocent," said Dove.

"James Louden has not come here to lose himself but to look for something, haven't you grasped that?" said Coffin irritably. "For him, innocence or guilt doesn't come into it just now. He's not interested."

The first news of James Louden came when he was seen leaving an eating house near London Bridge. The policeman on the beat recognised him, tried to follow him and lost him in the crowd almost at once.

Within a day his trail was picked up on a routine check of lodging houses in the district. He was staying in an old house near the river. This time there was a boy with him.

"The boy has been there all the time," said Dove. "He never went to Scotland. They parted in London and only Louden went home. That's how I see it. Now he's back. Thought you said he was looking for something?"

"He's found it," said Coffin.

"They'd cleared out by the time I got there. Had a quarrel. Do you think he'd hurt the boy?"

"Yes, I do," said Coffin. "If he could."

The third appearance of James Louden was on the Embankment. He was sitting staring out over the river, wrapped in oriental calm.

"It's all over," he said to the policeman who touched him on the shoulder. "I'm finished."

"You're on your own?" said Coffin, as soon as he was brought in.

"On my own and I'm empty," he drew out his empty pockets and let the linings flap.

"You've crossed a boundary then," said Coffin, recognising his state of mind.

"Yes. And now you've got to cross it too."

To be on the run successfully you have to be clever. You have also to be something close to a chameleon. Or if not a chameleon, anyway a little animal that is very good at hiding and changing its looks.

A large public lavatory stands near Creevey Park, which in turn lies behind Creevey Buildings. The sexes are divided by a large bare anteroom which is always empty. There are chairs but no one sits on them. Perhaps it would be a strange place to sit. Everything here is so clean, bare and impersonal.

A wiry figure wearing a longish raincoat approached the men's side, pushed open the door and disappeared. From the back it looked a boyish figure but with girlish undertones produced by the over-long hair and the soft coat. A great many boys wear long hair nowadays, though.

When the figure reappeared the hair was brushed forward and looked fairer and cleaner, and the coat was being carried over the arm.

With the difference in the coat and the hair a subtle change had come over the figure. There was a slight alteration in the carriage, a freer toss to the head.

From the back the figure looked more girlish.

By the time the walker was a hundred yards away the change was complete and it was now definitely female.

The girlish figure gave a little skip. It was away and free.

"Clever boy," said John Coffin, reaching out from the police car parked in the kerb and getting a firm

181

hold on the thin wrist. "Clever Joe Louden. I've got your dad here." And as the boy looked furious, he said further, "Well, I thought I ought to have somebody, you're a dangerous little fellow."

"He'd have killed me if he could," Coffin said to Dove afterwards.'

"He must have pretended to be a girl often enough before," said Dove. "That was how he got the room at Winnie Martin's. Her eyesight was poor, of course, but she saw in the end. Or else it was the sight of the handbags. I'm not quite sure which upset her first, poor old Winnie. He doesn't seem to know himself."

Behind it all was an obsession. An obsession with handbags.

"I couldn't cure the boy of it," the Indian doctor said, "although his mother brought him to me for treatment. But I could have sent him to someone who could. I never got the chance," he threw open his hands wide. "They never came again. Ah, there was hostility between them."

There was hostility between this boy and everyone thought Coffin, it flickered in and out of him like lightning in an electric storm. He was a chronic, compulsive hater. The obsession with handbags had only been the icing on the cake.

"Did you kill your mother because she wanted to cure your obsession? Or because you quarrelled?"

The boy did not answer. They were alone together in Coffin's room at his Divisional Headquarters.

"Don't try and tell me that you are mad," said Coffin gently. "Because you kept the money in the bags and used it, didn't you? It financed lots of things for you: the room in Mrs Martin's to begin with (although I doubt if you ever paid her much rent). So I'd call you practical."

The boy opened his mouth as if to start speaking and then closed it again.

"Yes, it would be practical to say you killed your mother by accident," agreed Coffin in a judicial manner. "But I doubt if that would hold for Winnie Martin, and to tell you the truth there might be other reasons against the killing of your mother being by accident. I don't think your mother went to that room in Creevey Buildings by accident. I think you took her there to kill her, and I think we can get the man who sells newspapers opposite to say he saw you there," he smiled at the boy. It was terrifying, he thought, to dislike and fear any boy as much as he did this one. "And then there's Sir Giles Almond in Murreinhead. He will probably be able to identify you. I suppose you attacked him just for looking round?"

"I never."

"What a liar you are."

"He never saw me."

Coffin smiled.

"I wasna there."

Coffin smiled again. Sweet little fellow, he was thinking, that's what we bring you up for, so that you can kill your mother and accuse your father.

He thought of his own child. Every family had its own tragedy, he supposed, so what was going to be his? Somehow he thought a version of Goldilocks and the Three Bears was more likely to be his story than this Oedipus-hate saga. A musical version, probably, with his wife singing all the best parts.

"It was my dad."

"I knew you were going to say that."

"You're clever, then."

"I can make you talk."

"You canna."

"Oh, yes, I can. I've got my own methods."

Joe stretched out an arm, which was blue with bruises. "Want to hit me like my dad?"

"I won't need to hit you."

"I'm too sharp to be caught that way, anyway," said the boy contemptuously. "Words don't count."

"You quite broke him up, you know. Accusing him of murdering Rina. He really thought you meant it. Until you took all his money and cleared out with it. He gave you up in the end. Like everyone does."

"I'm not loony, you know," Joe said suddenly. "You think so, but I'm not."

"Why should I think so?"

The boy was silent again.

"The handbags, perhaps?" prompted Coffin. "I've spoken to your doctor."

"My doctor. He's not my doctor." His voice was full of anger; he hadn't wanted to be cured, he liked his madness. "He thought I needed treatment. I only collect handbags. I *want* them. They mean something to me."

"I know. But you like to slash them too."

"Everyone has something. You probably touch lamp-posts as you pass."

"I don't."

"You've got *something*, then. You must have. You're just not admitting it. Perhaps you can't keep away from dust-bins," he gave a little giggle. "In a moment you'll be asking me how it started."

"I'd like to."

"Well, I shan't answer," he shrugged.

"I love you. I really do."

"Don't think I'll say anything, because I won't... Perhaps it started when I stole some money from Rina's handbag and he thrashed me. Rina kissed me but he thrashed me. I had a handbag of my own once but I don't remember that far back. I think it was a little red handbag, only he took it away from me and said handbags were only for girls. Anyway, that's what I'm saying. You can work out for yourself if it's true or not," he looked impudently at his questioner.

"It was clever of you to dress up like a girl. I expect you've borrowed your mother's clothes often enough before... No, you needn't say anything."

"Wasn't."

"It was clever too to use the room in Creevey Buildings: till you had something better like the room with Mrs Martin. How did you get to know about it?"

The boy just glared at him.

"All right, don't tell me. No doubt you had a lot of acquaintances (we won't call them friends, will we?) in that sub-world of yours, who could put you on to Creevey Buildings. I already know that you're a boy who can pick up ideas."

"I hate you."

"I know you do." Hate was standing out all over him like bristles. "Why don't you talk about it? You've already started. Why don't you tell me more?"

Joe did not reply.

"You'll feel better when you've told me."

"I feel good enough."

"I bet you do. Not for long, though. The night's coming, boy. And you've killed two women, one of them your mother."

"You'll never get me. Never."

Coffin smiled. "Want to bet?"

"You couldn't... I never left..." He stopped. His voice trailing away.

"Fingerprints? You never left fingerprints? No, you will be tried, but that won't be because of your fingerprints. You didn't leave any. Not in Creevey Buildings, not in Mrs Martin's."

"I'm not listening."

"No? I think you are, so listen hard." Coffin leaned forward. "There are sweat pores in the hand too. You left a palm print."

"It's all lies."

"Oh, pack it in." Coffin was not to be stopped now. "Shall I tell you what they'll do to you? You'll plead 'Not Guilty' but you'll be found 'Guilty.' You're only sixteen. They'll probably send you to prison. But don't worry: you'll be out before you're a grown man.

The boy turned slowly to face Coffin.

"And you know what I'll do the minute I'm out?" His lips were curved in a beautiful smile. "I'll kill *you*."

When is a case really over? Is it any easier to say that it is over than it was to know when it began? Did this one end when John Coffin knew logically who was guilty? Or when he obtained proof of guilt? Or when the murderer confessed? Which in this case he never did?

Or is it even when all the people concerned move on to the next episode in their lives?

In John Coffin's case this was soon; another death took place before the end of the week. He was soon busy looking for the murderer of two little boys.

James Louden went to sea, and as far as anyone knew did not see his son again. Joseph Louden will come up for trial next month.

So perhaps the case is not quite over. Perhaps it never truly will be.

In Murreinhead even Giles Almond soon found other preoccupations.

"Rina Louden being killed certainly let Lizzie Hamilton off the hook," said Giles to Santonelli.

"Don't you believe the boy Joe slashed the coat too then?"

"We shall always have to suppose so now. But I wonder…"

"You've got nothing against Lizzie except you don't like her."

"That's it."

"And you a lawyer!"

"Why did she need a dog leash?"

Santonelli started to laugh.

"She really has got a dog now. Or her husband has. He bought it. A whacking great Alsatian. And it can't stand the sight of Lizzie."

"So Lizzie's met her match said Giles, with satisfaction.

"And you know about Agnes Dyke?"

"No. What?"

"She went on and on about those ghosts until someone thought he would have a look round Alexander's rooms. He's got them full of rabbits. A score of them all lined up in hutches. He was keeping them as pets. It's against the Town Council regulations, you know."

"Agnes knew, of course."

"She knew all right. And that's why she created the whole episode. She was drawing attention to Alex's rabbits. She wanted to get him into trouble."

188

"And will he?"

"Why, no. Because it turns out they've really been married all these years, only they quarrelled. Now they're going to live together."

"So this was really Agnes's way of making up?"

"Ach, that's marriage," said Santonelli philosophically.

There was one genuinely happy ending. Lal Jennings could walk. Either the shock of Winnie Martin's death or the mere fact of her friend's absence, the withdrawal of the support on which she had leaned, had restored power to her legs. The muscles were weak and she could only go slowly. But she could go out into the world.

And to her joy, she liked it.

"It's a beautiful world. Brighter, rosier, cleaner than I remembered. Better and better. I love it," she said.

So perhaps this was the real ending of the case.

GWENDOLINE BUTLER
COFFIN IN
OXFORD

"It was like a Chinese puzzle. In St Ebbe's was a flat, in the flat was a trunk, and in the trunk was a body. The body of a woman..."

Ted was brought round from the first attack, if you could call it an attack, with difficulty. He had been found shut up in a cupboard with a scarf tightened around his neck: his own scarf, to add insult to injury...

THIS IS THE FIRST TIME in paperback for this novel featuring Gwendoline Butler's popular sleuth, John Coffin. The fact that Gwendoline Butler is one of the most borrowed authors in Britain will come as no surprise to her many readers. She is also one of the most universally praised, and with good reason. Recently voted one of the world's Top 200 crime writers, If you haven't tried Gwendoline Butler, why not start now?

'Gwendoline Butler is excellent on the bizarre fantasies of other people's lives and on modern paranoia overlaying old secrets; and her plots have the rare ability to shock'

—ANDREW TAYLOR, THE INDEPENDENT

Price: £4.99 ISBN: 1-902002-00-8
Available from all good bookshops, or post free from: CT Publishing, PO Box 5880,
Birmingham B16 8JF
email ct@crimetime.demon.co.uk

JENNIE MELVILLE

WINDSOR RED

CHARMIAN DANIELS, on a sabbatical from the police force takes rooms in Wellington Yard, Windsor near the pottery of Anny, a childhood friend. The rhythm of life in Wellington Yard is disturbed by the disappearance of Anny's daughter with her violent boyfriend. Dismembered limbs from an unidentified body are discovered in a rubbish sack. A child is snatched from its pram. Headless torsos are found outside Windsor.

Are these events connected? And what relationship do they have to the coterie of female criminals that Charmian is 'studying'...? All is resolved in a Grand Guignol climax that will leave the most hardened crime fiction fans gasping.

JENNIE MELVILLE is the pen name of bestselling crime fiction author Gwendoline Butler, one of the most borrowed authors in Britain under either name, and recently voted by *The Times* one of the world's top 200 crime writers. This is the first time in paperback for this novel featuring her popular Police Inspector, Charmian Daniels, one of the most universally praised of police procedural series, and the first to feature a female protagonist.

Price: £4.99 ISBN: 1-902002-01-6
Available from all good bookshops, or post free from: CT Publishing, PO Box 5880, Birmingham B16 8JF
email ct@crimetime.demon.co.uk